RYLAND'S REACH

Bullard's Battle
Book #1

Dale Mayer

RYLAND'S REACH (BULLARD'S BATTLE, BOOK 1)
Dale Mayer
Valley Publishing

Copyright © 2020

ISBN-13: 978-1-773361-95-6
Print Edition

Books in This Series:

About This Book

Welcome to a new stand-alone but interconnected series from Dale Mayer. This is Bullard's story—and that of his team's. All raw, rough, incredibly capable men who have one goal: to find out who was behind the attack on their leader, before the attacker, or attackers, return to finish the job.

Stay tuned for more nonstop action as the men narrow down their suspects … and find a way to let love back into their own empty lives.

His rescue from the ocean after a horrible plane explosion was his top priority, in any way, shape, or form. A small sailboat and a nurse to do the job was more than Ryland hoped for.

When Tabi somehow drags him and his buddy Garret onboard and surprisingly gets them to a naval ship close by, Ryland figures he'd used up all his luck and his friend's too. Sure enough, those who attacked the plane they were in weren't content to let him slowly die in the ocean. No. Surviving had made him a target all over again.

Tabi isn't expecting her sailing holiday to include the rescue of two badly injured men and then to end with the loss of her beloved sailboat. Her instincts save them, but now she finds it tough to let them go—even as more of Bullard's team members come to them—until it becomes apparent that not only are Bullard and his men still targets … but she is too.

Sign up to be notified of all Dale's releases here!
https://smarturl.it/DaleNews

PROLOGUE

BULLARD CHECKED THAT the helicopter was loaded with their bags and that his men were ready to leave.

He walked back one more time, his gaze on Ice. She'd never looked happier, never looked more perfect. His heart ached, but he knew she remained a caring friend and always would. He opened his arms. She ran into them, and he held her close, whispering, "The offer still stands."

She leaned back and smiled up at him. "Maybe if and when Levi's been gone for a long enough time for me to forget," she said in all seriousness.

"That's not happening. You two, now three, will live long and happy lives together," he said, smiling down at the woman he knew to be the most beautiful, inside and out. She would never be his, but he always kept a little corner of his heart open and available, in case she wanted to surprise him and to slide inside.

Then he realized she'd already been a part of his heart all this time. A good ten or fifteen years by now. But she kept herself in the friend category, and he understood because she and Levi, partners and now parents, were perfect together.

Bullard reached out and shook Levi's hand. "It was a hell of a blast," he said. "When you guys do a big splash, you really do a *big* splash."

Ice laughed. "A few days at home sounds perfect for me

now."

"It looks great," Bullard said, his hands on his hips as he surveyed the people in the massive pool surrounded by the palm trees, all designed and decked out by Ice. Right beside all the war machines that he heartily approved of. He grinned at her. "When are you coming to visit?" His gaze went to Levi, raising his eyebrows, then back at her. "You guys should come over for a week or two or three."

"It's not a bad idea," Levi said. "We could use a long holiday, just not yet."

"That sounds familiar." Bullard grinned. "Anyway, I'm off. We'll hit the airport and then pick up the plane and head home." He added, "As always, call if you need me."

Everybody raised a hand as Bullard boarded the chopper to the Houston airport. The chopper was Ice's, and one of her men would ride with Bullard in the copilot's seat, just to fly the helo back to the compound. Ice had volunteered to shuttle him there, but he didn't want to take her away from her family or to prolong the goodbye. He hopped inside, waving at everybody as the helicopter lifted. Two of his men, Ryland and Garret, were in the back seats. They always traveled with him.

Bullard would pick up the rest of his men in Australia. He stared down at the compound as he flew overhead. He preferred his compound at home, but, damn, they'd done a nice job here.

With everybody on the ground shouting their goodbyes, Bullard sailed over Houston, heading toward the airport. His two men never said a word. They all knew how he felt about Ice. But none of them would cross that line and say anything. At least not if they expected to still have jobs ... and jaws.

It was one thing to fall in love with another man's woman, but another thing to fall in love with a woman who was so unique, so different, and so absolutely perfect that you knew, just knew, you had no hope of finding anybody else like her. But Ice and Levi had been together long before Bullard had ever met her, which made it that much more heartbreaking.

Still, he'd turned from his view of Ice and looked forward. He had a full roster of jobs to focus on when he got home. Part of him was tired of the life; another part of him couldn't wait to head out on the next adventure. He managed to run everything from his command centers in one of two locations. He'd spent a lot of time and effort at the second one and kept a full team at both locations, yet preferred to spend most of his time at the old one. It felt more like home to him, and he'd like to be there now but still had many more days before that could happen.

The helicopter lowered to the tarmac, and he stepped out and walked across to where his private plane waited. It was one of the things that he loved, being a pilot of both helicopters and airplanes, owning some of both birds himself.

That again was another way he and Ice were part of the same team, of the same mind-set. He'd been looking for another woman like Ice for himself—but no such luck. Sure, plenty were around for short-term relationships, but most of them couldn't handle his lifestyle or the violence of the world that he lived in. He understood that.

The ones who did mostly had a hard edge to them, which he found difficult to live with. Bullard appreciated everybody being alert and aware, but, if some softness wasn't in the women, they seemed to turn cold all the way through.

As he greeted some of the ground crew, Ryland and Garret hanging back, Bullard finally turned to board his small plane and called out in his loud voice, "Let's go, slowpokes. We've got a long flight ahead of us."

The men grinned, confident Bullard was teasing, as was his usual routine during their off-hours.

"Well, we're ready. Not sure about you though," Ryland said, smirking.

"We were waiting on you this time to leave," Garret added with a chuckle. "Good thing you're the boss."

Bullard grinned at his two right-hand men. "Isn't that the truth?" He dropped his bags and said, "Stow all this stuff, will you? I want to get our flight path cleared and to get the hell out of here."

They'd all enjoyed the break. Bullard tried to get to the States once a year to visit Ice and Levi—and the same in reverse. But it was time to get back to business. Bullard started up the engines and got confirmation from the tower. They were heading to Australia for this next job. They'd refuel in Honolulu. He really wanted to go straight back to Africa, but it would be a while yet.

Ryland joined him in the cockpit and sat in the copilot's spot, buckled in, then asked, "You ready?"

Bullard laughed. "When have you ever known me not to be?" At that, he taxied down the runway. Before long he was up in the air, at cruising level, pointed toward Hawaii. "Gotta love the view from up here," Bullard said. "This place is magical."

"It is once you get up above all the smog," Ryland said. "Why Australia again?"

"Checking out that newest compound that I've had my eye on. Besides, the alpha team is coming off that ugly job in

Perth. No one left there to deal with. So we'll give them a day or two of R&R, then head home."

"Right. We could have some equally ugly payback on that job."

Bullard shrugged. "That goes for most of our jobs. It's the life."

"Don't you already have enough compounds to look after?" Garret asked.

"Yes, I do, but that kid in me still looks to take over the world. Just remember that."

"Better you go home to Africa and look after your first two compounds," Ryland said.

"Maybe so," Bullard admitted, "but it seems hard to not continue expanding."

"You need a partner," Ryland said abruptly. "That might ease the savage beast inside and keep you at home more."

"Well, the only one I like," he said, "is married to my best friend."

"Sorry," Ryland said quietly. "What a shit deal."

"No," Bullard said. "I came on the scene last. Clearly they were always meant to be together. Especially now that they're a family."

"If you say so," Ryland said.

Bullard nodded. "Damn right, I say so. Now to change the subject. Terkel contacted me."

"What did he want?" Ryland asked. "He's a strange one."

"He is, but when he speaks, I listen."

"Sure, I do too. But who understands what he says?"

Bullard burst out laughing. "True. It often sounds like he's speaking in riddles. This time, however, he was very clear. *An old enemy stalks me.*"

"That's nothing new. We have tons of those."

"Very true. But he was dead serious this time."

And that set the tone for the next many hours. They landed in Hawaii, and, while they fueled up, everybody got off to stretch their legs, walking around outside a bit. This was a small private airstrip, not exactly full of hangars and tourists. Then they hopped back on board again for takeoff.

"I can fly," Ryland offered, as they took off.

"We'll switch in a bit," Bullard said. "Surprisingly I'm doing okay yet, but I'll let you take her down."

"Yeah, it's still a long flight," Ryland said, studying the islands below. "What a stunning view of the area."

"I love the islands here. Sometimes I just wonder about the benefit of, you know, crashing into the sea, coming up on a deserted island, and finding the simple life again," Bullard said with a laugh.

"I hear you," Ryland said. "Every once in a while, I wonder the same."

Several hours later Ryland looked up and said abruptly, "We've made good time, considering we've already passed Fiji."

Bullard yawned.

"Let's switch."

Bullard smiled, nodded, and said, "Fine. I'll hand it to you." Bullard stood.

Just then a funny noise came from the engine on the right side. Followed by dead silence.

They looked at each other, and Ryland said, "Uh-oh. That's not good."

Boom!

And the plane exploded.

CHAPTER 1

R YLAND ROSCOE OPENED his eyelids to the brilliant hot sun above. He slammed them shut immediately, the dry salt making thick crusts on his eyelashes. He reached up his free arm, limp, probably broken, and slowly wiped his face. He eased over the massive pieces of debris that he'd tied together into a makeshift raft to check on his buddy. His good arm had an iron grip on Garret.

Ryland had lost track of time, the sun beating down hard on him, and the lack of drinkable water making this an endurance run. That he'd even survived the airplane explosion was one thing, but it was a separate one entirely as to whether he would survive this slow death in the sunny heat atop warm ocean waters.

In the distance he heard some shriek or a yell. Probably the damn birds again. Though most would wait until he died, a lot of them flew overhead on a regular basis to check to see if he'd moved. He'd lost track of time as he slipped in and out of consciousness.

When he heard another odd shriek, he lifted his head and blinked, then blinked again. A boat came toward him, some sailboat yacht-looking thing, but everything was blurred, and the size of it shifted in and out with his vision.

He kicked Garret in his unbroken leg, hard. "Garret, we got company."

Immediately Garret groaned and lifted his head. He stared and then he dropped his head back down again. "Good guys or bad guys?" he whispered in an equally hoarse voice to match Ryland's own.

"Well, I sure as hell hope it's good guys," Ryland said. "Just hang on there, buddy." They were both hurt, but Ryland was likely less hurt than Garret. His leg was at an odd angle, but thankfully it was a clean break and so far, there hadn't been enough blood to bring the sharks. He knew it wouldn't take much to lure them here, as a circle of them appeared when they initially came down, but so much plane debris was spread at least one mile across the oceans that they had soon lost interest.

"Ahoy, anybody alive?" she asked.

He slowly raised his injured arm and called out, "Yes!"

At that, he heard another excited shriek and before long the sailboat pulled up closer to his spot on the debris. A woman called out, "I'm throwing you a buoy—look for it."

He shifted as much as he could to see a swimming buoy tossed his way. He managed to snag it with his injured arm, wincing, but maintaining his death grip on Garret's belt. Ryland waited, balancing precariously on his floating home. They were slowly tugged toward the boat. He shifted as much as he could without bringing on the waves of pain waiting for him. "My buddy, he's hurt worse than I am."

The same woman calmly said, "Good to know. Can you help get him up?"

Ryland lifted himself up on his good elbow, not letting go of Garret, released the buoy from his broken arm, and gritted his teeth as he grabbed the side of the boat, his body screaming in pain. "Garret, come on, buddy. We've got to get you up and out of here."

Garret lifted his head and stared at him. "I'm here."

"I know you are, and I know you're hurt, but we've got to get you onto that boat." It was a painfully slow process, but the woman had surprising strength. She grabbed Garret's belt, and—with Ryland lifting and her pulling—they managed to get Garret's broken body up and over the side of her sailboat. The only thing that made it slightly more unmanageable was that Garret had passed out when first lifted. She slowly lowered Garret's head to the deck.

Immediately she looked over the edge of her sailboat at his floating raft and asked, "What about you?" Her gaze landed first on his arm, then traveled down that same side to his leg. "Jesus," she said. "Let's get you up here. Be careful. That leg looks pretty raw."

"The leg is a bitch," he said, "and the arm and ribs too. Everything on that side. But if I'm lucky, nothing else is too badly broken."

"What happened?" she asked.

"Plane exploded," he said in a curt voice because he knew that getting into the boat would be horribly painful. But he made it. He also knew his skin had gone ghostly white because he felt clammy, plus his voice faint after this exertion, but, when he finally made it to the deck of the sailboat, he whispered, "Thank God." Then he slowly passed out too.

The next time he woke to see the same woman, only this time she looked a little bit different.

He looked around and realized he was in a bed, most likely aboard her sailboat, as he felt the rocking motion of the ocean. "What the hell happened?"

"Oh, you're awake," she said. She walked over and held out a cup. "This is water," she said. "I want you to take a slow sip." He shifted up on his good arm and noticed that his bad arm was now in a sling. She held the cup to his lips, and he slowly drank. He wanted to grab the cup and toss it back, but she was portioning it out.

He glared at her.

She just smiled and said, "All in good time. We can't inundate your body all at once, but we need to get good fluids in there."

When he had slowly drank the full cup, he sagged back down and asked, "Garret?"

She motioned beside him, on the other side of the night table.

He leaned to see his buddy. "How is he?"

"He's alive but in rough shape," she said. "With any luck our signal for help will get somebody down here soon."

"Here?"

"We're just off one of the Micronesian islands," she said. "I was on my way to Thailand, when I was diverted by the plane."

"You saw it come down?" His tone sharpened, as he studied her with a little more clarity. "What did you see?"

"Just the plane nose-diving," she said. "Leaving a ton of smoke and fire in a trail behind it. I'm not even sure it was the landing that caused the breakup, as much as maybe you broke up just before you hit. It was really hard to tell, and it all happened so fast."

He nodded and said, "I know. It was pretty brutal. Did you see anybody else?"

"Nobody," she said. Realizing what he meant, she stopped, looked at him, and whispered, "How many more were there?"

"One," he said. "My boss and friend. His name is

Bullard. I'm Ryland. That's Garret on the other bed."

"I'm sorry," she said. "It's possible that he's been picked up by somebody else, but honestly I haven't seen too many people out here."

He nodded and sagged back. He would trust that Bullard was still alive because that was one tough-as-leather man. Sure, a blown-up plane could kill anybody, but, with Bullard, if there was any way for him to be alive, he would be.

Ryland looked himself over and then Garret. His friend was in a bad way, but at least he was alive. So was Ryland, and he'd place odds on Bullard being alive too. He better be. "How long before we can get to a medical facility?"

"Not exactly a traditional medical facility but we're sailing toward a US Navy ship," she said quietly. "They're coming to meet us."

"Good," he said. "Do they have a full medical center on board?"

"Fully state-of-the-art, yes," she said cheerfully. "The hope is to stabilize you both and then get you airlifted out."

"That would be nice," he said, and soon he was out cold again.

"IT WOULD BE nice, yes," Tabi whispered, brushing the hair off his forehead. What he didn't realize was that he was in worse shape than he probably knew himself. That leg would take some resetting, plus the gash on his head, his multiple breaks and cuts—they all needed attention. His whole body was black and blue. She had managed to strip him down— by cutting off his clothes—to see how much other damage there was, storing everything in a bag beside him. Not much of him escaped without some injury. She couldn't imagine the soft tissue damage inside. She didn't have any way to stitch him up, but he needed stitches—a lot of them—on multiple body parts.

Thankfully any blood had been cauterized by the seawater. Painful but effective in a pinch.

His friend had what appeared to be internal injuries too. He was the reason she headed as fast as she could toward the US Navy ship out there. It was just a sheer fluke that she'd seen the plane come down in the ocean and just another fluke that she'd found them floating among the debris. She'd been trying to get away from people, trying to get away from work, in fact trying to get away from everything. It had been a real shitty couple months for her, and this was supposed to be her time away.

But she never turned her back on anybody in need, and she'd never walked away from a natural disaster in her life. As a surgical nurse, she had heavy medical training, but she wasn't a doctor. Yet she'd seen some things in her time, and she knew critical injuries when she saw them, and this was one of those times.

Since finding the two men and making contact with the US Navy ship, she'd been looking for any other crash victims but hadn't seen any. Again what a fluke that she'd even seen these two. The floating pile of rubble had caught her interest, and, when she'd gotten closer, she thought she'd seen movement. Now she was damn grateful she'd done what she could, but, if the one died, she wouldn't be happy. She checked her radio and sent out one more message. "Ahoy, USS *Sand Egret*. One patient was awake and is now out cold again. Second one is still out cold."

"We're about forty-two minutes out," spoke the same

man again. "We've picked you up on radar."

"Good," she said. "I can't see any sign of you on the horizon yet."

"We're there and should be visible soon."

She kept going in the direction she needed to go, hoping the weather cooperated. She didn't like being out in the open seas as far as she was likely to be by the time they got the two men transferred. She could only hope that the weather, which had been threatening a squall all day, held off. The last thing those two needed was yet another event. She glanced around behind her to see a few other ships around where the debris field was—everything from scavengers to curiosity seekers. Hopefully somebody would see the third man. She didn't dare take the time or the energy. She had two critical patients on board.

It didn't take forty-two minutes; about thirty-seven minutes later the ship came around an island, and another ten minutes passed before a Zodiac raced out to meet her. As soon as one of the seamen boarded her vessel, she took him below and showed him the two men.

He was surprised. "Both white," he said. "Interesting. Did you get an ID from either of them?"

She pointed. "His clothes are in the bag, and that's his ID there."

He pulled it out and looked at it. "Ryland Roscoe. Africa. That's interesting," he said. "What are they doing here?"

"I don't know," she said. "Neither has been in any shape to really talk."

"We'll get them transferred up and out," he said.

She got out of the way, as the men carefully unrolled a portable stretcher and transferred Garret into it, still out cold. They moved him up and out onto her deck and then onto their Zodiac.

"Can you take both of them together?"

"We'll take this one first," he said. "Keep going in the same direction as the ship, and we'll meet you again."

She nodded and watched as they raced away. When she heard Ryland call out, she raced belowdeck to see him sitting up again, looking for a drink of water. She got the water, as he looked at the other bed.

"What happened to Garret?" he asked, his voice harsh. He tried to swing his leg over and cried out.

"Wait," she said. "The US Navy just came and took him to their ship. They could only take one of you at a time on the shuttle. You're next."

He looked at her, his gaze questioning. Then, after he finished drinking, he sank back and said, "Is Garret okay?"

"No, he's not okay," she said, "but he's alive."

"Good enough," he said, settling and wincing. "Damn leg."

"Yes, damn leg. It's broken."

"Dislocated for sure," he said, staring at it. "Maybe ankle and knee."

"You'll have to wait for the doctor on board to see," she said. She felt her boat starting to heave.

"What's the weather like out there?" he asked.

"Rough," she said, "but not too bad yet. A storm's been threatening for the last hour. I was hoping we'd make it to the ship, and I could get away before it got any worse." With that, she said, "I need to go back topside."

She headed up to the deck. They'd veered off course, and the wind had picked up. She shifted the mast, trimmed the sails, and corrected her course. The naval ship was off to the side but still a good distance away, and she saw no sign of the Zodiac. She could only hope that they would come back quickly. This was not the weather she wanted to be in out here, and she needed to head back to shore just as soon as she could.

The waves continued to pick up, and they tossed her small sailboat higher and higher. She knew she couldn't be out here much longer before she should turn around and cut for the coast. It didn't matter what the navy guy had said because, if they didn't get back here soon, she couldn't stay afloat and transfer the second patient.

Just when she thought it was time to cut for the coast, she looked out and saw the Zodiac. Suddenly a heavy gale came up, hitting her hard. Her little boat was tossed in the wind. When she heard a *snap*, she knew her mast was going. She cried out as it came crashing down. The Zodiac reached her within minutes. Four men hopped out, leaving the driver inside, and two of them went down to her visitor.

Two of the men came over to her; one assessed the damage to her boat and shook his head. "You can't stay on board," he said. "You can't get back to shore like this."

She glared at him. "I was trying to get back to shore with the second man, but you guys ordered me out here."

"And the weather changed," he said. "Go grab whatever you've got. She'll start taking on water soon."

"No," she said. "She's seaworthy."

"She was," he said. "But now she's taking a battering out here." He pointed out where the water sloshed over the sides, the lower cabin already filling up. "How is the bilge?"

"Not keeping up with that," she said.

She swore and looked at the mast, as another heavy wave came over and basically filled up the cabin beneath them. Shouts came from the men down below. They came up slowly, hanging onto the sides, carrying Ryland on a stretcher. As soon as they got him on the deck, they were hit with yet another wave. The Zodiac snapped free of her sailboat.

She realized that this rescue was no longer for one person but for two. She ran down below and grabbed her purse and a few things, including a few pieces of clothing, before one of the men grabbed her and pulled her up through the waist-high water onto the deck. She realized that her boat, valiant as it always was, had given up the ghost and was sinking.

The seaman grabbed her bag. "What kind of swimmer are you?"

"In a swimming pool, great," she said. "In this shit, not so much."

Nodding, he handed her a life jacket and hung it on her, then cinched her tightly into it. They were thrown a buoy from the Zodiac. They both jumped into the ocean, grabbed on to the buoy, and slowly the two of them were pulled toward the Zodiac. The injured man was already on board. She had gulped more water than air. Soaked and her teeth chattering, she was dragged in over the side of the Zodiac, and, as soon as she was in, the motor roared, and the vessel spun around and took off toward the naval ship.

She stared at her little boat, as it slowly went under. "Oh, my God," she said. "I can't believe that just happened."

"I'm sorry," said someone beside her.

She looked up; it was the injured man. She smiled at Ryland and said, "Two lives for a boat? Not exactly a contest."

"No, but if you hadn't been trying to save us," he said, "you wouldn't have been caught in this storm."

"Well, I couldn't get to the coast because of the debris field, not without getting too far out anyway," she said. "I had to check the movement I thought I saw among the debris because you were out in a more open current. So I managed to rescue both of you, but ..." She lost her words, as she stared at her boat.

"Maybe we can get you another one," he said.

She tossed him a half smile. "Wouldn't that be nice?" she said. "But I gave up dreaming a long time ago."

His gaze was steady as he studied her. "That doesn't mean that everything has to be a nightmare though," he said quietly. "Sometimes good things happen. And I do thank you, for my life and Garret's. I'm not sure how much longer we could have hung on out there."

"You were pretty well supported on that raft you managed to make," she said. "The problem would have been lack of water."

"Yeah, water, the heat, and the injuries," he said. "We might have survived a day, but I'm not sure Garret would have."

Thinking of the injuries she suspected both men had, she nodded, smiled at him, and said, "No, that's quite true."

They took another pounding as the Zodiac bounced from wave to wave, fighting the storm as it headed back toward the naval ship. It had been tough going even for this experienced crew. Now that seven were on board, the vessel was weighed down, and it would be a fight to get to where it needed to be.

She hung on tight, as one of the seamen signaled to her to check that her life jacket was on correctly. Gratefully she tightened the straps, noting that the injured man had been put into one as well. That wasn't a good sign, considering how difficult and painful that must have been. After losing her sailboat and now stuck in the middle of the ocean in a storm, hoping they could reach the naval ship in time, all helped to put the situation in perspective.

The seaman beside her smiled and said, "It's okay. We'll make it."

She gave him a disbelieving look. "We're taking on water too," she said, as the waves broke overhead.

"Yep," he said, "but we're used to it, and the ship is expecting us. So, if we have any problems, they'll come and get us too."

She let out a slow breath and said, "Well, that's good to know because this isn't exactly the way I pictured my life ending."

"No," he said. "One good deed deserves another. You saved the lives of two men, so don't worry. We'll make sure we get you out of here."

She gave him a bright smile and nodded. "They're missing another friend of theirs too," she said, motioning toward the plane's debris floating in the ocean.

He looked at her curiously. "Did you see anyone?"

She shook her head. "I wasn't even coming out to check because they were so far out," she said. "But I thought I saw movement, so I went to look. I'm sure glad I did."

"So am I," Ryland said from the other side of her.

After that, the wind picked up, and it was too damn hard to hear. The wind caught their voices and carried them off in the opposite direction, making it almost impossible to communicate. The loud whistle of the winds and the deafening roar of the waves were all they heard, as Mother Nature broke overhead, obviously in a tempest of some kind.

Tucking her head in against the edges of her life jacket, she curled up in the smallest ball that she could and closed her eyes against the wind and the water, wishing she were anywhere else but here.

CHAPTER 2

A HARD POKE had Tabi Sutherland lifting her head. The seaman beside her pointed, and she saw the side of the big naval ship ahead of her. She was stunned. It was just so massive as it rose above her. She was also numb from the cold rainwater. If she was expected to climb, they were out of luck; her limbs had stiffened in the cold. "Jesus," she said. "I didn't realize how big it was."

"It's pretty scary," he said. "Especially if you've never been close to one before."

When the Zodiac moved into the shadow of the big ship, she thought in her mind that the waves had increased just that much more. As they pulled up to the side, lines were tossed. They were snugged up close, but it was a challenge to get everybody up and off. This weather just added to it. By the time she stood on the deck, shivering from the cold and the wind, she was grateful to see Ryland being carried indoors. As she stood here, with the one lonely bag, purse inside, in her hand, she looked around at the wide-open space and the metal decking. "What do I do now?"

Just then a navy man in a white uniform approached. He smiled and said, "Petty Officer Joe Smithson. We have a room for you, but we'll get the doctor to check you over first."

She smiled. "I'm not injured," she said. "That was my boat that went under though, so I could really use a hot shower and a chance to dry off."

"That can be arranged. Follow me, please." She followed him down the stairs and through a long hallway until she was shown a small room. "This is yours," he said. "When you're done, we'll see you two floors up."

"Sure," she said, looking around the tiny-ass room. And just like that he was gone.

But then, what did she expect? It was a huge ship, and hundreds of people were probably on board. However, she was pleased to see she had a small bathroom all to herself. She stripped down out of her wet clothing and stepped into the hot spray, ever mindful of the water issue on a ship like this. As soon as she was clean and warmed up, she shut it off and grabbed the towel, dried off, and stepped out in the bedroom to get dressed.

The trouble was, the clothes in her bag—even though it was waterproof—weren't much drier than what she'd had on. She pulled them out and frowned. What she needed was something drier than what she had. When a hard knock came on the door, she grabbed a T-shirt, threw it on, and wrapped the towel around her. She opened the door a crack to see the same petty officer.

He said, "Here's some fresh clothes. Don't know that they'll fit, but they're dry."

At that, her face lit in delight. "Thanks, I was trying to figure out what I would do. The only change of clothes I had in my bag were soaked too."

"I'm not sure about your shoes," he said doubtfully, looking at her bare feet.

"I'm okay with wet shoes," she said.

"If you give me all your wet clothes," he said, "we'll get them dried for you."

"Perfect, just give me a minute." She closed the door and emptied the bag of clean dry clothes on her bunk. She tried on the clothing he'd given her. The pants were a reasonable fit. The shirt was tight across the chest, but it would do. She packed up all her wet clothing in the bag the seaman had brought her. Anything that was fabric she bundled up with her wet clothes. Dressed again, she opened the door. "My shoes are just soft canvas runners," she said.

He nodded, as she handed the bag off to him. "May I come with you now?" she asked. "I don't really know where I'm supposed to go." As she spoke, she quickly braided her long blond hair and brought it down around her shoulder.

He nodded and said, "I'll take you upstairs, where there's hot food and coffee waiting. Plus our captain wants to hear what happened."

"Of course," she said in a formal tone. Something was very odd about being in such a regimented area, where everybody else followed orders. But she didn't know which orders were hers to follow. So once again, she felt like a fish out of water. In this case, literally. As she followed him down the hallway and back up the stairs, she asked, "How are the two men?"

"They're in sick bay," he said. "I don't have an update yet."

"Right," she said. "Is it possible to see them?"

"It will be in a little bit," he said with a bright smile.

"Thank you," she said. "I really appreciate the navy's assistance. It was getting a little close for comfort out there in that storm."

"And I'm sure those two men you saved appreciated the

rescue too."

She laughed. "Hopefully, because, man, that was a rough go there for a while."

"I'm sure it was," he said. "We heard reports of the plane going down and knew we were the closest in the area, but we were still way too far out to save anybody in the short-term."

"Well, thankfully we're here," she said, "and that's the least of our issues right now."

"Exactly. Did you hear any of the details?"

"No, outside of the fact that they said the plane blew up, and, by the time they were hit, they barely had time to get out."

"When it's flying that low, it becomes quite a catastrophe just to stay alive."

"Well, it was, but thankfully they made it," she said. "Although they're missing one man."

"I know. The Coast Guard is out looking," he said.

"Good."

He led her to the mess hall. "There's hot coffee and tea here, if you want something."

She immediately reached for a cup and the coffeepot. Once that was filled, she snagged a muffin and said, "This will do for a start."

He just chuckled and said, "Dinner will be here in an hour or so." He walked her to where two navy men sat, both in uniform. Both men stood and shook her hand. She heard their names, but, at this point, names and faces were a blur, although one was the captain. She smiled when they asked her to seat herself, and she sat down. As soon as she sat, the men sat down too.

She appreciated the respect, although she suspected it was their training. She looked at the two men and said,

"Thank you very much for the help."

"Well, in this case, the rescuer needed rescuing," he said, "but that was partly on us. We couldn't get a second trip in fast enough, and we ended up sending you out farther into the rough water, which was not the right answer."

"It just seemed like you wouldn't make it back to get the second man, and I didn't want him to die."

"Understood. And much appreciated," he said.

Then the other man offered, "I'm sorry about your boat."

She winced. "Yeah, me too."

"Is it yours?"

She nodded slowly. "I've had it for quite a few years now," she said. "So it'll take me a bit to get over the loss."

"So where are you currently living?"

She realized they were asking for details about her that went beyond making conversation. "I'm a surgical nurse out of Perth, with odd hours, long hours, so don't get to sail as much as I would like," she said. "Plus, my boat is berthed in Sydney because my brother and I had a tradition to come out to these waters for years. Yet I have a friend whose boat is docked in Perth. So we kinda have a boat-share thing going. I've kept my boat here in Sydney and come out during my holidays."

"I'm sorry. This is not what you needed on a holiday getaway."

"Maybe so," she said. "But, at the same time, it is what it is."

They discussed her work, her life, and her holiday a little bit. She wasn't sure if they were prying or just trying to be friendly.

She asked, "What about the two men? Any chance I

could see them?"

"We can arrange that," the captain said, looking at Petty Officer Joe Smithson. "Get an update for us, will you?"

Immediately he rose and disappeared.

"It's the first man I'm really worried about," she said. "He was never conscious all the time I had him."

"I understood his condition is more severe," the captain said.

The petty officer returned a few minutes later. "The one is still unconscious. The second is awake, and, yes, I can take you down to see them."

With that, she stood, leaving her empty coffee cup and the muffin wrapper behind. With a smile, she said, "Thanks for the coffee and the snack."

"Dinner is in an hour," the captain said. "Not to worry, we'll make sure you're well fed."

"And then what?" she asked curiously. "Do I get a ride back somewhere?"

"Yes, as soon as the weather calms down," he said. "We'll fly you to shore, if we can't take you, or we'll send you on by boat."

"That would be much appreciated," she said. Then she turned and followed Joe. As they walked, she asked him, "Did they get any details on the first guy? Like what his injuries are?"

"If they did, they didn't tell me," he said.

She fell silent after that because, of course, it was all about hierarchy here and the need to know. She had dealt with the same in the hospital. As it was, even with her escort, she got completely lost getting to the sick bay area. They had stairs and hallways and more hallways and more stairs. "How do you not get lost in these ships?" she muttered.

He laughed. "It takes a bit to get used to, but most of them are built in a fairly similar way. So, once you've been on one, you're pretty good at understanding how the others work."

"Says you, but, at least if I go on a cruise ship, diagrams are on every landing," she complained good-naturedly. "Here? I haven't seen anything to tell me where I am, just a series of numbers and letters."

"The numbers and letters indicate your levels and whether you are forward or aft," he said. "What's located on each floor isn't something that we post."

"You probably should though," she said. Just then he turned and went through a set of double doors. She followed behind to a medical center. It was funny how they immediately went from one to the next, and it didn't seem to matter whether you were on a ship or in a hospital. It looked like a fully functional medical facility, and she instantly felt at home. Several men stood off to one side.

The petty officer cleared his throat, and the men looked up. He said, "This is the woman who came on board with us along with those two men."

One of the doctors walked over, frowning. "Are you hurt?"

She shook her head. "No, just heartsick that my boat went under," she said with a laugh. "How are the two men I picked up?"

"You picked them up, huh?" She nodded. "I'd love to know more about what you saw when you found them," he said.

"Why?" she asked.

"Just to see the kind of injuries they may have. We're taking x-rays and doing a full workup on the unconscious man right now."

"That's Garret," she said. "How is Ryland?"

"Ryland is awake and will probably be happy to see you. We've popped his leg back into place. He's got a couple hairline fractures and a lot of soft tissue damage that he'll notice for the next month and a half," he said with a smile, "but we don't have to do any surgical intervention for him."

"Well, that's good, except for what? Two hundred stitches?"

He laughed. "Yes, it was about two hundred, now that you mention it. Good guess."

"I'm a surgical nurse," she said.

He looked at her with interest. "Good to know. I may need your services while you're here."

She looked at him in surprise. "Why is that?"

"We're not happy with Garret's condition, and I may need to go in and take a look. Normally I'd send him out on a helicopter, but, with the weather right now, we're not flying."

Garret, although he was safe, was not out of danger by any means.

RYLAND HEARD THE voices in the other room. He was hoping he heard the voice of the woman who had plucked them out of the ocean. It was a woman for sure and sounded like it could be her. He tried to look through the glass pane to his doors, but some film was over it, giving him an unclear visual.

Just then the double doors opened, and the doctor walked in. "You have a visitor," he said.

Sure enough, it was her.

She walked up to him, a big smile breaking across his face. "Hey, I'm so glad to see you looking better."

"Well, yeah, considering most of the breaks aren't major," he said. "Also they got my leg put back in place, so I'm feeling a whole lot better than I deserve to be."

"Isn't that the truth," she said, nodding. "But you have a lot of soft tissue damage."

"Always," he said. "Just like any explosion, you take a blow like that in the sky, and then you fall into the water, which is another hard-impact injury. It's not easy."

"You did have a chute on your back, didn't you?"

"We did, and it slowed the plummet but didn't stop it because we were too close to the ground."

"Understood, but, outside of a few breaks, dislocations, and over two hundred stitches," she said with a laugh, "how are you feeling?"

He gave her a big grin. "I'm alive," he said, "and I'm pretty thankful for that, all things considered."

She nodded. "Your friend is still unconscious and in serious shape," she said quietly. "They're running him through a bunch of tests, but they're afraid that they may have to open him up to see what's going on."

"Well, at least we're here in a safe place with specialists on hand."

"They'll try to get us off here," she said, "but a hell of a storm is brewing."

"Exactly. That's how these things go," he said. "Well, you and I are safe and sound, so it comes down to whether or not they can handle whatever Garret needs."

"We won't know just yet."

Ryland nodded and smiled. "How did you happen to be out there in the middle of the ocean?"

He listened while she told him about taking time away from her job at the hospital in Perth. "It's always been a favorite holiday destination," she said, "so I kept my boat docked in Sydney."

"I'm sorry to ruin your holiday," he said, and he really was sorry. That was shitty for anybody, and he hoped like hell she had insurance on her boat, but he didn't have a clue how that worked.

"It is what it is," she said.

Something in her tone suggested a lot more was going on in her world than she'd shared, but then why would she tell him? "We were heading toward Australia to pick up the rest of our team," he said. "I need to contact them." He sat up and looked around. "I guess there's no phone or anything that I could use to call them."

Now that he had a good chance to study her, he saw the high cheekbones and the clear blue eyes, her wet hair now braided down the side. She was tall, trim, and dressed in a shirt obviously a little too small across the chest, but provided a delightful strain on the buttons, and pants that somewhat fit. "I gather your clothes were soaking wet?"

"Everything I have is soaking wet," she said. "I don't know if my phone survived or not. I left it in my room."

"I need to get a message out to the guys. They were expecting the plane."

"Well, if you give me a number to call ..." she said, looking around for something to write it down on. Not finding anything, she disappeared out into the main room.

He collapsed back, taking several deep breaths because, damn, he was really sore.

When she returned with a small notepad and a pen, he wrote down the number and said to contact Cain.

"Okay, what am I to tell him?"

"Just tell him what you know—that the plane exploded midair, that you rescued the two of us, but we … we're missing Bullard." At that, his voice cracked. She looked up at him, but he just sighed. "He's a good friend … and my boss."

"Will do," she said and then hesitated. "Anything you need?"

"They're bringing me soft food," he said. "I'm getting IVs for liquids and vitamin shots, so I'll be fine. What about you?"

"I'm supposed to get dinner in an hour, and there was talk of flying to land," she said, "but I think, with the storm, if they can't get you guys out, chances are they can't get me out either."

"No," he said. "It's all about safety for the crew and the passengers."

"Understood," she said, as she smiled and patted his hand. "I know that you're pretty banged up, but you're lucky to be alive."

"And I'm alive, thanks to you," he said softly.

She looked down to see where she patted him. "I'm sorry," she said. "OMG the skin has been flayed right off you."

"Wouldn't be so bad," he said, with a note of humor in his voice, "but after they flayed the skin off me, they dropped me in saltwater."

"Ouch," she said with a laugh. "Mother Nature was a bitch today."

"Maybe she had good reason," he said. "I wish I knew what made the plane go down."

"Did you have any warning?"

He shook his head. "No, we were just coming in and

maneuvering a better position. We weren't even very far out anymore. We were at the end of a very long flight, coming from Texas in the US. We had stopped in Hawaii to refuel."

"And it just happened, at the very end?"

He nodded.

"Bizarre," she said. "Anything suspicious about it?"

His gaze narrowed, as he studied her. "I don't know," he said. "Outside of the fact that the plane went down from an explosion, which is always suspicious."

"Right," she said. "Not that I know anything about it, I just wondered."

"And with good reason," he said quietly. "The thing is, I don't know. Until I can get back on my feet, I don't have any idea what happened, but I will find out."

"Well, you're not getting on your feet for a little while," she said. "So give up that idea."

"Oh, I'll be up pretty damn fast." She frowned at him, but he just gave her a crooked grin. "It's hard to keep me down."

"I know guys like you," she said. "Big and tough until something bigger and tougher knocks you sideways, and then it's even harder to get you back on your feet." She shook her head. "Even the big guys drop. And sometimes harder than they expect."

"I know," he said, "but the longer I sit here and think about it, I'm worried about the rest of my team. Because, if we were targeted, maybe they are in danger too."

She stopped and stared at him. "Targeted? Your team?"

He shrugged. "We run an international security company, and Bullard's the head of it. We're stationed out of Africa, but we work with other companies around the world. One of them is in Texas, and, in our line of work, we've made some pretty big enemies."

"Oh," she said, studying him with alarm. "Like enemies who would blow you out of the air? That kind of enemies?"

"Enemies who would blow us out of the air and leave us to die in the ocean. Absolutely," he said. "You can bet that I'm already plenty pissed that there's no sign of Bullard around. Because if they took him out ..." With that, his voice trailed off, as he thought of what would be the repercussions of something like that.

"Well, don't even start thinking along those lines," she said, reaching out to softly grab his fingers. He looped his fingers with hers. "You first have to heal."

"I do," he said, "but then? All bets are off."

"Well, there's nothing you can do while you're here, so relax," she said. "You need your strength."

"Go make that phone call for me, will you?"

"I'll see what I can do," she said. "I can't guarantee you that my phone works at all. But the navy should be sending out messages from here to whoever you need, to let them know that they've picked us up."

"Well, I know that the alerts have likely already gone out," he said, "but that doesn't mean anybody in my group knows."

She frowned at him.

"Please," he said, his voice steady and low. "It's important."

CHAPTER 3

J UST SOMETHING IN the tone of Ryland's voice worried Tabi, as she walked down the hallway, hoping she would find her room soon. As a sailing enthusiast, she had a very good sense of internal navigation, but this ship was giving her fits, and she'd already had to backtrack several times. But she was determined to see if her phone would work. His words had already been enough to send her hustling out of there. But the doctor had again asked her on the sly if she was available, in case he needed a hand.

"Absolutely," she said, "but don't you have a half-dozen people here ready and able to do this?"

"Maybe," he said, "but we've also got two down in sick bay. And this isn't something I want to start with somebody green."

"Got it," she said. "If you need me, I'm there." She just hoped that it didn't happen. It was one thing to be a surgical nurse in her nice perfect hospital, with a system that she understood, versus being here, dealing with something that was much more an off-the-cuff emergency surgery. But, because it was an emergency, she would help in any way she could. That didn't mean it would be easy though.

Finally she stopped and stared at the room in front of her. She thought it was the right one. She quickly unlocked it and stepped inside, relieved when she saw her personal belongings on the bed and only hers. She hadn't even considered that she could be rooming with a second person here. This was not a world that she wanted to live in. And, therefore, it wasn't something that she touched on very often.

She walked to her phone, where she'd taken it apart and pulled out the battery, so it could all dry. Checking it, she realized it was pretty dry to the touch and popped it back together. She turned it on and actually had power. She quickly dialed the number Ryland had given her and waited for someone to answer.

"Identify yourself."

Surprised for a moment, she replied, "I'm Tabi Sutherland, calling on behalf of Ryland Roscoe."

There was a short silence on the other end, then he asked, "Where is he?"

"We're both aboard a US naval ship," she said. "Their plane was blown out of the air, and he and Garret managed to survive long enough for me to pick them up on my boat. We were heading toward the navy ship, when the weather came up. I have since lost my boat and am on board the naval ship as well."

"Condition?"

Almost like a military drill, his clipped tone gave instructions for further information. "Garret is bad," she said, not mincing words. "Likely internal injuries. They're still assessing him. Ryland also has probable internal injuries, but nothing requiring surgery. He's got several fractures, multiple stitches, and a dislocated leg, knee, and ankle, but he will survive. I believe his forearm on the right side is fractured, and he has several cracked ribs. In addition, he has some vertebrae damage, but he's not talking about that."

"That sounds like Ryland," the man said, relaxing slightly. Then came another hesitation. "No sign of a third man?"

"If you're asking about Bullard, Ryland said to tell you there's been no sign of him that we're aware of, but the Coast Guard is searching."

"Damn."

"He said something about you and the rest of his team needing to know that," she said. "They're getting excellent care right now."

"Got it," he said. "Do you have a location?"

"I can give you where we were," she said, "but I can't tell you where we are now because I don't know our ship's longitude and latitude."

"We'll find it."

"If you say so. If you've got a way to get us off of here, you may want to pull some strings and make it happen. You also need to watch your backs, Ryland says. He thinks you might be in danger."

"We'll handle it. And we can get you off," he said easily, "but we don't want to cause any more damage to our friends' condition by doing so in the meantime."

"Then wait," she said. "At the minimum, we need to find out how badly hurt Garret is."

"Right. And we have your number," he said and quickly repeated it back.

She frowned and nodded. "Yes, that's quite true." She added, "I'm a surgical nurse just recently out of Perth. I was on holiday on my boat."

"We appreciate you picking up our friends," he said, his voice much warmer. "Your good deed will not go unnoticed."

She laughed. "And neither is anything required," she

said. "I just want to get home safe and sound."

"Understood. We'll stay in touch." And, with that, the voice at the other end of the phone disappeared.

She put her phone on Vibrate, just when a knock came on her door. She almost wanted to groan because, so far, this place had been people upon people. She wouldn't say anything, but the whole point of her holiday was to get away from it all. She opened the door to see the same petty officer waiting for her. She smiled up at him. "Is it dinnertime?"

"It is, indeed," he said with a smile.

She pocketed her phone and said, "I'll keep this with me, unless I'm not allowed or something."

He shook his head.

"Good," she said. "I contacted Ryland's friends at his request, to let them know where he and Garret were. I'll need to see him again after dinner."

"If you remember the way, you can go right after dinner. And ask the doctor about times when the sick bay is open, so you'll know when you're allowed to be there," he said with a cautionary note.

"Right," she said. "I don't know how anything on board works."

"And nobody expects that you should," he said, "but, if you have any questions, feel free to ask, and I'll do my best."

"Right," she said. "I appreciate the dry clothes."

"Even with the wet feet?" he asked, looking down at her shoes.

"Well, at least they're canvas," she said. "By morning, they'll probably be dry."

"If you give them to me," he said. "I'll make sure they dry overnight. We can toss them in the dryers."

"I imagine your washing machines here are a fair size."

"They're huge," he said. "Also lots of them."

"I imagine so," she said. "I appreciate the dry clothes and the fact that I'll be getting my others back. A good night's sleep will show me a whole different world."

"It will, indeed," he said. "And hopefully the squall will have passed as well."

"I was calling it a squall when the winds came up," she said. "I think we're well past that now."

"It is pretty rough out there," he said.

"And yet this ship is so big, we don't even notice it."

"Maybe that's a good thing," he said with a smile, "But even she can get to rocking when it gets bad."

"Well, I'm glad it's not bad yet then," she said, laughing. "I'm not sure I have too much interest in seeing it get bad …"

"Interest?"

"No, I didn't mean it that way," she said, laughing. "Just that, I don't want to be out in the storm anymore. So, if I get to enjoy a nice quiet sail until we're back on shore, that suits me."

He said, "A word of warning, it'll get noisy when we go up to dinner."

"Right. Does everybody eat at one time?"

"No," he said. "We run shifts here, like everywhere else."

"Sounds good," she said. "I'm really hungry."

He stood in line and introduced her to the seamen working the line, as they went through getting food. By the time she had a full tray of roast beef, mashed potatoes, Yorkshire pudding, gravy, and steamed vegetables, she was in awe. "I can't believe you can eat like this."

"Good food is part of keeping a happy crew, you know? It's how a system like this works," he said. "Just imagine the dissension we would have if nobody was happy with the food."

"I guess," she said, shaking her head. "It's amazing."

He escorted her to an empty table and said, "I'll get some juice and water. Can I get you one?"

"Yes, please, to both." She waited, looking around to see a few curious gazes sent her way, but generally everybody ignored her as they went about eating their food. But then they probably only had a certain amount of time before getting back to whatever work they had to deal with. Ships like this had to be run with an exact schedule, to keep things from coming apart.

She was amazed at the number of people here and how seamlessly everything seemed to run. By the time Joe returned, she'd already dug into her food. When he set the juice down in front of her, she looked up, smiled, and said, "This is delicious."

"Good," he said. "I'm glad to hear it. I'm really hungry myself."

She took a sip of her water too and looked around. "Does everybody know about the rescue that happened today?"

"Sure," he said. "Plus, there are announcements. We do take part in a lot of rescues. So, although it's a major traumatic event for you, it's commonplace for them. No offense intended."

She laughed. "No. Of course not. I understand." As she finished off her plate, she sagged back and said, "You don't realize just how much a home-cooked meal like this really hits the right spot."

"Especially when you're tired, cold, injured, traumatized, in shock, and—" he just continued to list off various states.

"Right," she said. "I did see some dessert up there."

He looked at her in surprise and said, "Go. Help yourself. By the time this lot has been through it, there won't be any dessert left." He added, "Would you mind grabbing me another bun, so I have something to sop up this gravy?"

She agreed and made her way back to the lineup and picked up a bun for him and a huge piece of chocolate cake for her. It had some hot liquid center to it. She wasn't exactly sure what it was, but it looked delicious. At the drinks station, she grabbed coffee for the two of them and came back. "I didn't know if you wanted a coffee," she said, "but I decided I'd grab you one just in case."

"Ah, thanks for that," he said. "I'll be nice and walk you back to the medical bay afterward."

"And that's why I did it," she said with spirit. "Because, Lord knows, it would take me forever to find it on my own."

He laughed. By the time he was done, and she'd finished her coffee and dessert, the room had more or less emptied.

"Wow," she said, staring around. "That's an awful lot of people in and out in a relatively short time."

"Yep," he said, "but we all have a purpose."

She nodded and waited until he had his dessert.

At that point he said, "Come on. Let's go. You're getting antsy."

She smiled and asked, "How can you tell?"

"Could be your fidgeting," he said.

Indeed, she was playing with the handle on her coffee cup and moving the cup around in gentle circles. She laughed. "The things you don't realize you do, until it's pointed out to you."

He hopped up, and together they carried their dishes over. He showed her how to sort through and distribute the trays and the dishes. Then he led her outside the dining room. "Everybody has to help keep their corner of the world as clean as possible around here," he said. "There are too many of us, and it all piles up if we don't."

"Hey, I'm all for it," she said, laughing, as he led the way through the ship again to the sick bay. This time, she tried to memorize how to get there from the mess hall.

He turned and said, "By the way, if you need a snack or something hot to drink later tonight, you can come back up and get it. There'll always be something."

"Good to know," she said. "Hopefully, once I get to bed, I won't budge until morning."

"I hope so," he said, then pointed up ahead to the double doors. "I'll leave you here. I have to report to my duty officer."

She smiled and called out, "Thanks." Pushing open the doors, she headed into the calm atmosphere of the clinic. One person was in attendance at a desk on the far side. Tabi lifted her hand and said, "I just came in to see Ryland."

"Are you okay to go in on your own, or do you want me to go with you?" the woman asked.

She looked at her in surprise. "I'm fine to go in alone, assuming he's awake. I don't want to wake him up, if he's getting some rest."

"I think he's awake. He just finished dinner not too long ago."

Tabi nodded, walked to his room, and called out softly, "Ryland, you awake?"

"Yes, ma'am," he said.

She stepped closer and saw a table with an empty tray and dirty dishes sitting beside him. "I just finished eating too," she said with a smile. "Did you enjoy it?"

He nodded and smiled. "It was good. Nothing like a warm tummy."

She nodded and smiled. Pulling her phone from her pocket, she said, "It works."

His face lit up. "Did you contact them?"

"I did," she said. "So they know about you and Garret, and I told them that there was no sign of Bullard."

He nodded and sank back. "Thank God for that," he said. "Did they say anything else?"

"No, he just asked me a bunch of questions about what I knew, where I was from, things like that," she said, with a shrug. "Honestly they seemed to be more interested in knowing what happened to the plane and what happened to you and, of course, how bad Garret was."

"Of course," he said, with a note of satisfaction. "They're not only my team, they're my friends. Obviously they're concerned about us."

"Well, now they know," she said. "I doubt there's anything they can do, but, if there is, I'm sure they're on it."

He rolled his head toward her and smiled, as he said, "You can bet your ass they're on it all right."

THAT WAS EXCELLENT news about Tabi getting the phone call through to Cain. Ryland had been wondering, worried about how to get a message out that he and Garret were alive and that Bullard needed to be searched for. He had to be out there somewhere. Bullard was a tough one, and Ryland would not mark him as missing or dead at this point in time.

Just because nobody knew where he was, well, that was often Bullard's way. The fact was, as far as Ryland was concerned, the plane crash was sabotage, and he knew that

Bullard would immediately be considering that himself. That fact alone created a lot more reasons why Bullard would likely stay under, if he'd survived.

Their debris had drifted a long way, spread out over at least a one-mile-long area, with the tides spreading it even farther. It would have been pretty damn easy for Bullard to not see them either. As it was, it was good news all around.

He looked at the woman who had rescued him and asked, "I don't suppose you'd make another phone call, would you?"

She nodded. "Of course," she said. "What number?" she asked, as she pulled out her phone. He read off the number, and, when a woman answered at the other end, he reached out a hand.

Tabi handed over her cell, and he said, "Ice?"

"Hey, Ryland. How was the trip?"

"A little rough," he said. "We were blown out of the sky. Garret is badly hurt, and Bullard is missing. Garret and I are on a navy cruiser, out in the middle of the ocean."

There was a short gasp and then a moment of silence.

He winced, remembering the relationship that Ice had with Bullard. "I'm sorry," he said regretfully. "No easy way to tell you something like that."

"No," she said, her voice faint, before it strengthened and became brisk. "Do you have the coordinates?"

"I have the approximate coordinates, where we went down, yes," he said. "Where we're at right now, I'm not sure. I know that the US Navy is getting ready to get us off here, depending on the weather. We're in the middle of a big storm."

"They'll wait for morning," she said. "You're safe where you are, and, unless Garret needs emergency surgery that they can't provide on board, they'll probably keep you there."

"That was my take too," he said. "I don't want to think about Bullard hanging on to a piece of plywood out in the middle of the ocean, like we were."

She paused, then asked, "How badly hurt are you?"

"I don't deserve to be alive," he said boldly. "But I'll be honest and say the damage, though it'll hurt like shit for quite a while, is rather minimal. My right leg was dislocated at the ankle and knee joints, several fractures on the tibia, right arm, and a couple fingers that I don't know if they even x-rayed or not, but they're probably broken. Still, not a whole lot we can do about it." He held up his right hand and twisted it around, noting how much swelling was going on in his fingers. "The back, a couple ribs—you know." He tried to pass it all off.

Her tone was very sympathetic when she said, "At least you're alive. And Garret?"

He heard the note of fear in her voice. "He's alive," he said softly, "but he's in bad shape. I know one of his legs was looking beyond rough, but it's soft tissue damage that I'm really worried about. And the fact that he hasn't woken up, from whatever knocked him out. Well, I'm afraid of a brain injury."

"If anybody can pull out of it, it would be Garret," Ice said. "Is a doctor there for me to talk to?"

"I don't think so," he said, looking around. He held a hand over the receiver and asked, "Is a doctor here? Ice is looking for an update on Garret's condition." He watched as Tabi walked through the double doors out of his room and told Ice, "Tabi has gone to see if anybody is out there at the moment."

"Tabi?" Ice asked curiously. "Navy?"

"No," he said. "Angel."

She gave a snort at that.

"I'm not kidding," he said. "She saw us on our makeshift raft. I don't know how. Probably from the birds flying above. She was out sailing and came to check it out and managed to save the two of us. Then headed toward the navy ship that met us, and they managed to get us to the ship via a Zodiac, but the storm really came up in between the two trips to get us both off. She lost a mast, and then her boat went under. It's all the navy could do to save her at that point in time too."

"Damn," Ice said. "You've really been in hot water, haven't you?"

"Icy, freezing cold water actually, but yes," he corrected. "When I get back on my feet, I'll do something about her boat."

"And I'm sure you'll get lots of help with that from the rest of us," Ice said swiftly. "Anybody who does a good deed, like saving the two of you, deserves at a bare minimum to have her property replaced. Did she get hurt?"

"No, I don't think so." But he stopped and said, "Shit. You know what? I didn't even ask her."

"Well, you probably should," she said, with a note of humor. "When you get guardian angels like that, it's always a good idea to keep them in good shape, well rested, and knowing they're appreciated, in case you need them again."

"True enough," he said.

Just then Tabi walked back in and shook her head.

"No, on the doc right now," he said into the phone.

"Fine," Ice said. "I'll go through official channels and get it within the next hour anyway."

He had no doubt about that. "If you find out something, let me know."

"And how would you like me to do that?" she asked.

He winced and said, "This is Tabi's phone. You could always send her a text message, at least over the next twenty-four hours maybe, while we're both confined to the ship. I have no idea when we'll hit land, so I don't know what we're doing after that. Tabi was on a holiday, and honestly I'm not even sure what part of the world we'll end up in."

"Good point," she said. "Maybe Perth, depending on where you're traveling right now," she says. "I've got you heading toward Australia."

"We were flying over the Micronesia Islands."

"Maybe," she said. "This computer, although it's supposed to be updated, is plotting the coordinates a bit off. Probably due to the storm. I'll find out for you."

"Thank you," he said. "And Bullard?"

"You know me. I scuttled up to send a crew while we were chatting," she said. "We're on it." And, with that, she hung up.

He laughed and returned the phone to Tabi. "There's nobody in the world like Ice," he said, in admiration.

"Your girlfriend?"

He looked at her in surprise and then smiled. "No, she's married to another good friend of mine," he said. "But they're two peas in a pod, and I'm absolutely delighted. Actually I find that my faith in human relationships centers around what they have," he admitted. "And I don't mean to be metaphorical or anything, but what they have between them is very special. And they're all good friends, even better friends of Bullard's," he said sadly.

"Well, there's no way to know yet about Bullard," she

said. "You survived, so there's a good chance he did too. That debris was scattered a long way."

"Well, I'm really hoping so," he said, "and I know, if anybody out there will get to the bottom of this, it'll be him."

"And you," she said shrewdly.

He frowned. "And here I was thinking I could hide that need to get answers from you," he joked.

"No point," she said. "Besides, why would you want to? If somebody blew you out of the sky, then it's pretty damn obvious you'll want to find out who it was."

"Exactly," he said. "And that's a hard place to even begin investigating from, as evidence is streaming across the ocean, especially when I don't even know where the hell I am, in terms of my physical condition."

"Actually I'm surprised you're even allowing that to stop you from thinking along those lines."

"I'm not allowing anything to stop me," he said, feeling his irritation grow. "But stuck out in the middle of the ocean on a naval vessel limits my options, you know?"

"I guess it depends on how badly hurt you are," she said, studying him.

"Besides, I'm not sure I want to leave Garret."

"And sometimes we have to," she said gently. "Just because there's no way not to."

He frowned and then gave a clipped nod. "If there was a way to go back, I would."

"Can you think back to how somebody could have planted a device like that?"

"We stopped in Honolulu for gas," he said. "So it's quite possible, but I'm not sure that it was then. It could have been planted before that, even in Texas."

"And triggered how?"

He gave her a hard look. "In this day and age, a phone call could have triggered it."

"Did you hear a phone ringing?"

"It didn't have to be up in the cockpit with us," he said quietly. "Triggers are tiny, and a cell phone could have been put in, close to where the bomb itself was."

She crossed her arms and stared at him. "The back end appeared to blow from my vantage point. So it would have been someplace around the back section of the plane, I would think."

"And that's important too," he admitted. "Only three of us were on the plane, when we stopped for fuel. It could have been on the outside of the plane. We did get off and walked around to stretch our legs a bit and checked a few things, but I certainly didn't go under the tail end, and I didn't see anything suspicious on the inside."

"But how big would it have to be?"

He frowned, thinking about that. "Not very," he said. "Probably the size of a fist would have done it, if it were placed properly."

"So then, depending on how it was covered up," she said, "it could have been disguised quite well."

"Unfortunately it was," he said.

"So now that you have some idea of *what*, you really need to know now the *why*."

"And," he snapped, "I need to know *how*."

"What would that give you?"

"Hopefully the person on the other end. The son of a bitch who placed that bomb."

"Do you have that many enemies?"

"Yes," he said. "And I don't regret any of them."

"I don't understand," she said. "Isn't that something you should regret?"

"No," he said. "That is definitely not something I would ever regret. Every enemy I've made was because I was helping the good guys take down the bad guys. But bad guys tend to have very long memories."

"Ah," she said. "Are you military? Or special ops or ... something?"

"Or something, yes."

CHAPTER 4

T
ABI WAS BACK in her room and had gotten a good night's sleep. She woke up, was currently sitting in her bed, wondering what time breakfast was. On a ship this size, she imagined it had already started. More sleep was impossible. She'd gone to bed early last night, after meeting and talking with Ryland, and even now she wanted to pick up coffee and take it to the sick bay so she could sit down and visit with him again. She knew that, as soon as they got to land, chances were, they'd be separated.

There was just something about him. Maybe it was the connection over having saved his life. Maybe it was the connection with almost having drowned with him. She didn't know, but something was very compelling about him. Besides, she really wanted to check on Garret. But she also felt like she needed an excuse to go. Just then her phone buzzed. She checked out the text and smiled; it was a perfect opportunity to pass on news to Ryland.

She dressed quickly into her cleaned and dried clothes, which she found when she got back last night, folded on her bed. So, back in civilian clothes, with dry shoes this time, she made her way out of the room and slowly, carefully, proceeded to the mess area. She was delighted when she found it on her first attempt. As she walked in, a good thirty-odd sailors were dotted around at the tables. She didn't see any breakfast food out yet. She walked over and asked somebody.

"They'll have the hot food out in fifteen," he said. "There's coffee, snacks, muffins, oatmeal, fruit, and things like that over on the sideboard."

She nodded, then went over and grabbed two coffees. She put cream in hers and left the other one black. Just something about Ryland made her think he'd take his coffee black. Then she moved out, as other people came in. Getting from the cafeteria back to the medical unit was a trick in itself, but, when she finally saw the double doors up ahead, she sighed with relief. She pushed open the swinging door, using her hip and shoulder, and walked on in.

The person she'd seen last night wasn't here. Instead a doctor stood here with a clipboard in his hands. He looked up and frowned.

She smiled. "I came to deliver coffee for Ryland," she said. "I have a message for him as well."

He walked to the door where Ryland was and checked, then said, "He appears to be awake, so go on in."

"Thank you," she said, then stopped and looked at the doctor. "Any update on Garret yet?"

"No," he said. "Not yet."

"There was some suggestion," she said, "that my services might be needed, if you had to do surgery."

"Ah, you're the surgical nurse. Chances of that are not good," he said. "At least, not at the moment. As long as he's holding on, we'll leave him as is."

"No swelling on the brain?"

He looked at her, smiled, and said again, "He's holding on, and we're keeping an eye on it."

"Well, if it hasn't gotten bad by now," she said, "chances are you won't have to open him up." And, with that cheerful note, she walked into Ryland's room.

He shifted, startled, and, when he saw her, his eyebrows rose. "What's the matter, can't sleep?"

"Well, I slept solid when I first went to bed," she confessed, handing over the coffee and placing hers down on the night table at his side. "And then I woke up, thinking about Garret and the one doctor saying they might need my help in case of emergency surgery. But I just spoke with the doctor outside, and, so far, that's not the case."

"If it would be needed, wouldn't it have happened already?"

"Yes," she said. "It's more a case of the brain swelling at the moment, I think."

She watched the wince on his face, and she nodded. "The brain is by far the biggest worry. Any internal bleeding must be abating, or they'd have gone in by now, and it's something they can monitor."

"Great," Ryland muttered, as he shifted in his bed, the sheet falling to his waist. She looked away, reminded of how incredibly muscled and well-defined his build was. Granted, she had seen all that when she had cut away his clothes, but she was worried about saving him at that point. In her job as a nurse, she'd seen an awful lot of topless men in her life, and a ton of them in hospital beds, but this was the first time she'd reacted this way. Then again, she wasn't on duty, and she was visiting somebody.

She motioned at the fresh stitches across his shoulder and more down the right side of his rib cage. "I see they did a lot of work on you."

"Quite a bit, yeah," he said. "Everywhere. I'm not even sure I can sit in this position very long."

She smiled. "Your butt did take a beating."

"Well, let's just say, it's not quite as nicely rounded and plump as it used to be."

At that, she burst out laughing. "I hardly doubt anything on you was plump," she said.

He grinned at her. "You never know."

She just shook her head. "Pretty damn sure." Just then she remembered her excuse for coming. She pulled out her phone and said, "By the way," as she brought up the text message that she'd received and passed her phone to him.

He looked at it, made a small sound of delight, and said, "Now that's more like it." He looked at her and asked, "Is it okay if I answer?"

She nodded her reply, and he quickly typed out a response. When he handed the phone back, he said, "So I'll be leaving here damn soon then," with a note of satisfaction in his voice.

She looked at his heavily bruised and marked-up body and asked, "Are you sure you're ready?"

He looked down at his most recent injuries and said, "Nothing here is major. Whereas, trying to find the trail of what went wrong *is* major, and the fresher the trail, the better."

She shook her head. "You can't go after them right now," she said. "You're too banged up."

"Nothing is broken badly," he corrected. "And the stitches will heal in a couple days, and the skin will close."

"You look like, well, Frankenstein," she said bluntly.

He looked at her, startled, then burst out laughing. "Thank you," he said, with a big grin. "I don't think I've ever had a compliment quite so nice."

She rolled her eyes, crossed her arms over her chest, and said, "It's not smart. Really. You should wait until next week.

At least until the stitches come out."

He gave her a hard look and said, "Not happening."

"What about Garret?"

"He's coming with me." He stopped, looked at her, and said, "You want to come too?"

"Where to?"

"We're heading to Perth," he said.

She nodded. "Then I'm definitely coming because that's home."

"What about your stuff at the hotel?"

"I was staying with a friend," she said. "I've already contacted her and let her know what happened. I used to live in Sydney and kept my sailboat there until I decided if I was staying in Perth long term or not."

"And you don't need anything from there?"

"I have my bag with me, so I have my basics. She'll just pack up any of my clothing there and store it, until I go back again. Most of my things were in the boat."

"Oh, sorry. Well, hand me your phone, and I'll make sure there's room for you on the helicopter." She watched in surprise as he immediately sent out another text and shifted in bed. He looked around and said, "I need food."

"I think breakfast is about to start," she said. "When I walked through, getting coffee, they said fifteen minutes."

"Good," he said. "We could be off of here in two hours." He looked at the clock over on the wall and said, "If not earlier."

"You must have friends in high places."

"That I do," he said. "So I suggest you go pack. I don't know if the doctor will release me to get my own breakfast though. I'm starving and don't really want to wait until somebody decides to collect me a plate."

"How about I get you a plate instead?"

He looked at her, assessing the offer. "I need a lot of protein, and, I mean, *a lot*."

"Tell me what you want," she said, one eyebrow up. "If I have to make two trips, I'll make two trips."

He grinned. "You know something? I like your style."

"Your style isn't too bad either, Ryland," she said with a laugh. As soon as she heard his breakfast order, she just shook her head and said, "Most doctors would kill you for eating all that or would think your arteries would kill you."

"Protein is very necessary to rebuild muscle," he said. "And I've got to have energy to go on."

"So you need carbs too."

"Absolutely," he said. Just then the doctor walked in. Ryland looked at him and said, "Any chance I can go get food?"

The doctor shook his head.

"Any chance I can go get him food?" she asked.

The two looked at the doctor expectantly. He raised his hands in surrender. "You seriously that hungry?"

"Absolutely," he said. "I'm starving."

"Well, that's a good sign. I'll do my checkup, if you want to get him a tray," he offered.

"Done," she replied and immediately spun on her heels and walked out the door. Now a little more familiar with the pathway, it seemed like it was half the distance to get back to the mess hall. Once there, she got a tray, two plates, and headed toward the hot breakfast selections. There she grabbed him a stack of pancakes, loaded up the eggs, sausage, bacon, and ham. Then, on the other plate, she added more bacon, ham, and sausages. She placed syrup on the side, along with butter, juice, coffee, and a glass of water. She then added several muffins, so he could have something set aside, in case he got hungry in a little while.

Her tray was extremely full, and she moved very slowly, heading toward the medical center. She had to pull off to the side, when several people passed, because she was worried about dumping her load. Eventually she made it back to the medical center and pushed open the doors. When she walked in, the doctor took one look and said, "Oh, good, you'll stay and eat with him."

"Not likely," she muttered under her breath.

But, as she headed toward Ryland, he was sitting up, looking like he was in a slightly less-painful position. She smiled. "What did he do, give you a shot in the butt for the pain?"

He grinned. "I wish that's all he'd done." Then he took one look at the plates and the tray in her hands and said, "Wow, you know how to follow orders."

"At your command," she said.

He reached out and moved the little hospital table across his lap, and she placed her very heavy load down.

"I'm sorry," he said. "I didn't think about how heavy that would be for you."

"I'm the one who said I could make a second trip, but then I got stubborn and put it all on one tray," she said with a laugh.

"How about you get your breakfast," he said, "and come back and join me? Another hospital table is over there. We can bring it here, so you can sit and eat too."

"I'll do that," she said, with a smile.

As she turned to leave, and the doctor walked in, he took one look at the two plates before Ryland and said, "I thought she was here to have breakfast with you."

He grinned. "Nope, this is all mine, and I'll be a while, eating it," he admitted.

"Back in five," she said.

She hoped nobody noticed, as she walked in with another plate on a tray, but nobody said anything, if they did. She quickly loaded up about half the mountain of food that he had, but she was terribly hungry too. With her full load and another cup of coffee, she walked back again, realizing just how many miles she was getting on this ship. By the time she walked in and sat down, she said, "I'm tired now."

"It's a lot to get used to, when aboard a navy ship, isn't it?"

"It is," she said, as she adjusted the tray table height, so that she could sit down and have it in front of her. She then picked up a sausage and bit into it. "What is there about a hot breakfast?" she wondered.

"Something very soothing to the soul," he said, "about any hot meal. But, when you're stressed and tired, it's the best."

"And I love breakfast anyway," she said. "So there's that."

Only silence came for a time, as the two of them worked their way through the breakfast. Just when she was finished, and he was two-thirds of the way through his, the doctor walked back in and said, "Good, you're almost done."

"Is our ride here?" Ryland asked, lifting his gaze.

The doctor frowned, nodded, and said, "I'm not sure how you managed it, but your ride will be here in twenty."

She immediately stood and said, "That's my signal to go grab my stuff."

"Meet right back here," the doctor said. "The three of you are leaving from here."

"Be back as soon as I can," she said, leaving her dishes behind.

RYLAND WATCHED HER go, appreciating her trim figure, as she bolted out of here. He understood how tired she was with her two trips to the mess hall. Life aboard a naval ship was something to get used to—the size of a ship like this and how many miles you actually log as you traverse it, from one end to the other. And she'd been doing the stairs a lot too.

The doctor motioned at Ryland's two plates and said, "I figured one of those plates was for her."

"Nope, both for me," he said, as he worked away on the pancakes, thoroughly enjoying getting tanked back up again.

"How did you manage the ride?"

"Pulled a few favors," he said. The doctor's manner was a little stiff, and Ryland wondered if he'd stepped on his toes. "Sorry," he said. "We've got emergencies happening all around, so I'm needed out of here. Not for lack of good care by any means," he said hurriedly.

The doctor relaxed a little bit and said, "I'd feel better if Garret were in a place more suited to his injuries. We've got state-of-the-art equipment, but that head injury concerns me."

At the mention of Garret, he was wheeled in on a hospital bed to join Ryland in his room.

Ryland looked at his friend, ever silent, and nodded. "That'll be the first thing we run tests on."

CHAPTER 5

A S SOON AS Tabi got back with her bag, she found Ryland already on his feet and dressed, with the gurney moving Garret to the upper deck. Ryland stood at the doorway waiting for her. He motioned at the gurney and said, "Come on. We're behind him."

She slowed her pace to get behind him, until he glared at her. She shrugged and moved forward. "Don't be so touchy," she said. "I'm not the one with stitches in my ass and everywhere else that could be slowing things down."

"Ha," he said. "My butt is just fine."

"It's more than fine," she said, laughing, but she deliberately didn't hold open the doors he went through either. Didn't want to set off his touchy ego again.

He just glared at her. "You could at least help," he said, in that mocking aggrieved voice.

"And get dirty looks? Nope, you're one of those big tough guys." She smiled. "You'll make do on your own."

By the time they got to where they were going, which was up on deck, a huge military helicopter waited for them.

She just stared at it in surprise and looked at him. "Is this your ride, Ryland?"

"Yep, and yours too," he said, as he grabbed her hand. "Come on." And, together, the two of them walked closer.

"I've never flown in anything like this," she said nervously.

He looked at her, squeezed her fingers, and said, "Stick by me, and I'll get you there safe."

"You're the one who was just blown out of the sky," she said.

He burst out laughing. "True enough," he said, "but that wasn't our fault."

"Says you," she replied.

But still, she followed his lead, and, by the time she was up in the helicopter and sitting down, he was working hard to buckle her in. Then she caught that slight grimace on his face as he pulled on muscles that had been stitched together.

"Sit down," she scolded. "I can do up my own buckles."

He sat down beside her and said, "Touchy, touchy."

"Not so touchy," she said.

"It's all good," he said, and he settled back with a smile.

She looked over, and her gaze caught on his strapped-down friend. "No change in Garret's condition, huh?"

Ryland's face was grim, as he shook his head. "No, none."

"I'm sorry," she said.

"It is what it is for now," he said. "This is a wait-and-see deal."

"Still, I'd rather get him back to a hospital," she said. "And wait and see there."

"That's what the doctor just said too, not that they don't have the best equipment, but, as you know, any serious cases like this? They lift off the ship anyway."

"Well, let's hope, when they run the tests at the hospital, they find something different."

"It may be that he just needs time."

"At least all the time he's been laying here, the injuries

have been set and closed off," she said. "The rest of him will heal."

"There is that," he said. "I have any number of fractures that need to heal myself."

"You're lucky no plates were needed."

"I wouldn't be ambulatory if that were the case," he said. "It felt more like I had been shaken hard, like a pill in a bottle, before being tossed in the ocean."

"But that landing was damn hard too. I know the chute didn't help much, but at least it was something."

"It was," he said. "Just not enough."

At that, he fell silent, and they stayed quiet, as the helicopter finally lifted. She stared out the window, amazed at the view below her. "And clear weather," she said. "It's absolutely stunning. But, in a storm like we just had, it's pretty ugly."

"It is, indeed," he said. "Mother Nature always reminds us who is boss out here."

"You were flying in good weather?"

"We were," he said. "So, no lightning strikes messed up the instrumentation."

At that, she looked at him. "Was there an instrumentation issue?"

He shook his head. "No, not at all. It just went from one minute to the next and then *boom*."

"Damn," she said. She looked around at the empty helicopter. "I thought your friends would be on here."

"They'll meet us on the next flight," he replied.

"This flight must cost a fortune," she said, tentatively worried that she might get dinged for some of it herself.

He looked over, smiled, and said, "Had to pull a favor or two."

"Friends in high places again."

"We need them sometimes in my line of work," he said, settling with his head back, resting. "Rest. You didn't get a ton of sleep last night."

"I slept well," she protested, but, as she looked at him, she saw the color leaching from his skin. "But you need to rest, yes," she said, as she sank back and stared out at the beautiful scenery around them.

"Don't let me sleep longer than thirty minutes," he murmured.

She checked her cell phone and said, "Done."

The next thirty minutes passed, with a sense of surrealism. The helicopter itself was high-tech, huge, and just had that power and authority of military. She loved it, but it felt very much like a foreign experience, like she was a little bug in a very big system, and she didn't really count for much, but somebody had decided that she should get this ride. It was pretty amazing, and, as long as she didn't think about her beloved boat, life would continue to be amazing. But that boat had been a long part of her life, her history.

She'd sailed it with her younger brother for years, until he had passed away from leukemia. She'd named it after him—*Lucas's Light*. And now, like him, it had been crushed under the pressure of Mother Nature's heavy hand. She wanted to be bitter; she wanted to rail at the elements, but there was absolutely no point. Just like her brother's death, the death of her sailboat seemed almost faded already.

She didn't even know if she wanted to replace it at this point. Lately it had seemed so much harder to get there for her holidays, and looking after it had become a pain—like trying to find a place for *Lucas's Light* after her friend Maureen's place had gone out of business for a bigger development to move in on the waterfront property. It just seemed like life was so much like that. Now Tabi had decisions to make, but at least she had her personal stuff with her, and her girlfriend would pack up and leave her little bit of clothing there. But it felt weird, like part of her was gone, a part of her history. And that hurt even more.

"What are you thinking?" he said, interrupting her thoughts.

"That you should be asleep," she said, with some asperity.

"You were thinking too loud," he murmured.

"I'll tone it down then," she said drily.

He snickered, kept his eyes closed, and shifted ever-so-slightly. She'd seen his body and knew just how much damage there had been. Hitting the surf and whatever debris had sliced into his body left tiny little knife cuts. It had to sting and hurt like crazy, but he'd suffered in silence. Stoic. But given the kind of work that he must do, she understood.

She'd seen big men like that come through surgeries all the time, but she'd also seen them on the other side, when they woke up with limbs missing or reattached or major breaks fixed, their bodies absolutely shaken and brutalized by what had to happen in order to make them better. She'd seen the tears in their eyes and the depression sink in, when they realized something worked—or didn't. It wasn't an easy thing to be bigger than life and stronger than what you thought the world should be.

But it was all about being true to who you were, and she appreciated it when the big men would also cry because of their pain or be depressed in their anguish. It wasn't good to keep it all inside. And she wasn't sure what the guy beside her was like, but, so far, Ryland had a sense of humor and an inner strength that she appreciated. She'd seen it all in her work.

And, just like that, the flight was over. She was shocked and sad, when they came down for a landing on top of the hospital, because the view, the scenery had been just so spectacular. With a start, she realized that she'd let Ryland sleep past the thirty minutes. When she reached out and placed a hand on his arm, gently avoiding his stitches, he opened his eyes immediately. His bright deep-green gaze came instantly about to stare at her. Not with the sleepy awareness of somebody just coming out of a nap but fully alert.

"Are we there?" he asked, his voice ever-so-slightly thick.

Relieved to see even some symptom of a normal person coming awake, she nodded. "We're just coming down on top of the hospital."

"Good," he said. "We need to make sure Garret gets the treatment he needs."

"I see people down there," she said, looking out the window.

"Cain will be there," he said, absolute certainty in his voice.

She said, "Cain? The guy I called for you?"

He smiled. "My friend and teammate."

"If you say so. Doctors and nurses are waiting for Garret too."

"Yeah," he said. "That's all part of it. Hopefully Cain will have news on Bullard."

"I hope so, for your sake, but I think you're asking a lot of your friends."

"No," he said. "I'm not. I'm not asking anything from them that they wouldn't ask of any of us."

"All hard-asses, are you?"

"Yes," he said, with a smile. "Definitely."

As it was, the chopper slowly descended onto the rooftop. When it came to a solid landing, she looked at him and said, "Well, for better or worse, we're here."

The doors were flung open. Ryland, knowing how to unbuckle, stood up. She struggled with the closures on hers. He reached over, brushed aside her fingers, quickly unbuckled her, picked up her bag, and said, "Let's go."

A tall man stood on the tarmac, right below the chopper, waiting for them, who looked like serious business. His face was hard, scars visible on his forehead, and he had the same build as Ryland. She looked at him, looked at Ryland, and asked, "Cain, by any chance?"

Cain broke into a big grin that flashed across his face, and he said, "Now that's my boy. You go out. Your plane goes down, and you come back with a beautiful woman."

Blushing, she stared at him in surprise, but Cain already had his hands around her ribs and had dropped her gently onto the concrete beside him. With that, Ryland, albeit a little slower, made his way out of the helicopter too.

Garret was transferred onto a gurney on the rooftop, and nurses and doctors carefully maneuvered him inside. With Ryland grabbing her hand and pulling her after him, she walked at his side and asked, "Now what?"

"I'm not sure. I'll need to debrief with Cain."

"Is this where we part ways?" She needed to bring it up because, well, he hadn't. But it felt odd, like she'd spent just enough time with him that he half belonged here, at her side. But she didn't really know who this man Ryland was. Looking at Cain, she asked, "Any word on Bullard?"

His face locked down, and he shook his head. "Not yet.

We're still looking."

She slowly nodded. "I remember what it was like out there," she said. "Bits of debris as far as I saw. It's only because these two were higher on the surface that I actually caught sight of them. Then, as I got closer, I think Ryland moved."

"Yep, that would be him, flagging down the prettiest woman in the area."

"In this case, the only woman," she said drily. As soon as they stepped inside the hospital, she felt that welcoming sense of familiarity to the atmosphere. "If they see me, they'll put me to work," she complained lightly.

Cain looked at her and asked, "You work here?"

"I'm a surgical nurse," she said. "I'm on holiday and still have another five days to go, but they're always short-staffed, so—"

"If you want, we can give you cover, right to the front door, and you can duck back out again."

"I want to see what's happening with Garret."

"Well, that's where we're heading right now," he said.

They made their way behind the gurney, and, as she walked in, Dr. Stevenson looked up and asked, "What are you doing here?"

"Well, it's a long story," she said. "I'm the one who picked these two guys up from a plane crash in the ocean. I was sailing nearby, and we ended up on a naval ship, and now I'm here."

He gave a snort. "I'm pretty sure you headed out for a holiday, so you didn't have to deal with all the trauma that keeps coming through here."

"Well, I was looking for peace and quiet, but I didn't quite find it. I ended up losing my boat in the storm, so now

I'm here," she said. "No, I'm not looking for work. I need a few days."

"No doubt," he said. "What do you mean, you lost your boat? Are you saying that *Lucas's Light* is gone?"

"Yes, while trying to reach the naval ship, a storm engulfed us, broke the mast, and she filled with water." It felt very prophetic to have to say that.

He looked at her, reached out, and gave her shoulder a light squeeze. "Sorry, kiddo. I know it meant a lot to you."

"Yeah, it did," she said, "but apparently it's time to move on. How is Garret?"

"I got his records earlier, so I've had a chance to study up. We'll run some CT scans and an MRI to make sure we don't have anything else going on." He looked at the two men with Tabi and asked, "Who are you?"

Ryland identified himself; Cain stayed silent. When the doctor looked at him, he raised an eyebrow and said, "I'm in charge of these men."

"Right," Dr. Stevenson said. "It'll be at least two hours before I get any information."

Cain looked at his watch and said, "You sure that won't be one hour?"

"I'll do what I can," he said. "No promises." He looked at Tabi. "Why don't you take them to the cafeteria, until I get some results."

"Good idea," she said. She looked at Ryland and said, "Come on. Let's get you some caffeine and some more food. It's been at least an hour since you ate."

He looked at her, laughed, and said, "That means there's at least a corner I can fill."

She just rolled her eyes, looked at Cain, and asked, "Do you eat like he does?"

The corners of Cain's lips kicked up. "Sometimes," he said, "especially when we're injured or when we're building muscle, then maybe."

She led the way to the cafeteria, which actually had fairly decent food and also had a nice open space, with lots of places to sit. She walked up to the front and grabbed a tray. Looking at the food, she shrugged and said, "I really don't need more food, but I sure could use some coffee."

She watched as Cain grabbed a couple sandwiches and two muffins.

"There's hot food too," she murmured.

"This will do for the moment," he said. "I'll get a steak in a couple hours."

She just gave a headshake, looked at Ryland, but he was mulling over the sandwiches himself.

"Ryland, there is more hot food, if you need it," she offered, not that she had any idea where he could possibly put it.

"But sandwiches can come with me," he said. He grabbed several, added some muffins and a couple power bars. Cain paid for it all, and she led the way to a table over on the far side. As soon as she sat down, Cain approached, looking around, then shook his head and pointed to another table that had nobody around it.

She shrugged, picked up her tray, and moved. "Why is this one better than that one?" she asked in a low voice.

"Nobody can hear us," Ryland said.

She thought about that for a moment and said, "Right, apparently that's necessary right now."

"It is," Ryland said, as he looked at Cain and asked, "Do you have any news?"

"The question is," he said, "what news do you have for

me?" With that, he gave a hard look at Ryland.

RYLAND GAVE A clipped nod and proceeded to explain the last few minutes on the flight. "We had no warning," he said. "We were just about to switch places. Bullard had insisted on flying most of it but didn't want to land, as tired as he was. I would bring it down. I was just about to stand up and move into the pilot's seat when the back end blew up. At that point in time, there was no taking over anything. Bullard had still been standing and got sucked out, so I'm not even sure exactly where he went down. Garret was there, still sitting in his seat, and he had parachutes for us. I managed to grab one and got sucked out, but I pulled the chute, and Garret did too. With him up there beside me, we were both free and clear, but we were too low. So the chutes weren't pulled fast enough, and we hit hard."

Taking a drink of water, Ryland continued, "I came to the surface and managed to get out from under the rubble and found a piece of debris to climb on, while I searched for Garret. I found him by his chute, and he was already under. I don't think he was under for long though because he was still struggling to survive. However, by the time I got him free of the parachute and up on the plywood, he didn't make a sound anymore. But he was breathing, so I laid him out as best I could with his injuries and looked for more debris to pack up into a bigger floatation area," he said. "No sign of Bullard."

"So, he had no parachute?"

"I'm not sure about that," he said. "I didn't see, and I haven't asked Garret. Bullard was in the process of going to them anyway. So it's possible."

"Knowing Bullard, all kinds of things are possible," he said. "He also would have been a little bit higher up, having gone out at the time he did."

"The plane just exploded. It broke up as soon as it hit, but it kept going for a while, so the debris field was pretty long."

Cain pulled out his phone and quickly sent a message.

"What are you doing?" she asked curiously.

"Having them push the debris field search perimeter back a couple miles to the other side of where it first started. If Bullard came down there and had a parachute, it's quite possible he did survive."

"But how would he have gotten a parachute if it was blown out before him?"

"There's all kinds of ways to maneuver in the air," Ryland said. "If he saw one that he could get to, he could dive toward it. Once he's got a parachute, then it's a whole different ball game."

"True enough," she said. "Did you actually see another parachute?"

"I didn't have a chance to see behind me at all," he said. "What I saw was Garret, and I was trying to keep my eye on him, so I could get to him. Although I was injured from the blast, I wasn't nearly as bad as he was."

"Right," she said, thinking about it. "I just can't imagine, what that was like, when you both were badly injured."

"I wasn't really injured yet at that point," he said. "So I was trying to get as close up to Garret as I could, just in case."

"Right, it was the landing that destroyed you."

"Some of it was probably from the plane, but I don't remember any of it. Maybe shock hid that part." He looked down at the long line of stitches on his forearm. "Like this. I have no idea how this happened."

"When a situation like that occurs," Cain said, "you react. You don't have a chance to think. You don't have a chance to do anything but move. So it gets to be fairly chaotic, and your only mind-set is to get through the motions of what you need to do in order to survive. In this case, I presume you angled as close as you could to Garret."

"I did. He was hanging in his chute, but I wasn't sure if he was just dazed or what because, when I found him in the water, he was conscious enough to be struggling."

"The cold water probably hit him and woke him up," she said.

"Woke him up and knocked him out," Ryland said, with a shrug. "I just hope there aren't any serious brain injuries."

"Now what about in Hawaii?" Cain asked.

"You'll need to check the airport cameras," he said.

"We already did," he said. "We saw two men close to the plane. One fueling the plane and another one talking to him. Wore mechanic's overalls. We have images of you, Bullard, and Garret getting off and going back on again. We're not seeing anybody else around the plane."

"I've been racking my brain since I woke up here," he said. "Trying to figure out where and when somebody could have planted a device. What about in Houston?"

"We're still looking for better video feeds of the plane. It's not great there."

"It's a massive space, and we weren't allowed to park too close to the hangar because it was overcrowded."

"Always," Cain said. "That airport is not exactly easy in, easy out."

"But it's the only other option, isn't it?" she asked him.

"Well, if we rule out Bullard committing suicide, and Garret and Ryland here doing a suicide-murder mission, then yes," Cain said. "We didn't see any cause for alarm in Hawaii, and that was a short stop. But the plane was in Houston for what? Four days?" He turned to look at Ryland.

Ryland nodded. "Five nights, four days," he said. "We got in the night before, close to midnight."

"Right. I remember that," he said. "I was here in Australia, and we sent another group back to Africa."

"How is the rest of the team?"

"Shocked," he said. "Everybody has high hopes for Bullard, as we all know how tough he is, but we also know that not everybody can dodge a bullet every time."

"He's beyond the nine lives of a cat too," Ryland said.

"Well past," he said, "but we're not going there yet."

"Good," Tabi said, with added force to her word. "I've seen people come through all kinds of circumstances. And just when you think it's already too late, they pull out, and they do just fine. Then I've seen what looked like the biggest, strongest men, who, all of a sudden, die. Sometimes there's no rhyme or reason to it."

"We've all seen cases where, against all odds, somebody has survived something they had no business surviving," Ryland said. He looked at Cain. "Where did you start?"

"Our viable threats folder," he said almost absentmindedly. "We're tracking down sixty-two men right now."

She whistled. "You've got that many enemies?"

"Way more than that," Ryland said, with a snort. "But those are the ones they've determined to be viable in this instance."

"How do you come off as being still *viable* or not?"

"Well, that's where the problem comes in," he said.

"Everybody else on the team is working the computers right now, trying to locate these sixty-two men and see who's involved in what."

"But still, if they hired somebody?"

"They might have hired somebody, but, chances are, it'll be one of their team. All these suspects are either teams or solos."

"Solos?"

"Men who have a personal grudge against Bullard, men who may have lost their entire teams, men who may have done time and escaped or are still in prison."

"Jesus," she said, and she shook her head. "That's unbelievable."

"It's the work we do," Ryland said. "Remember? We chase down the bad guys."

"Sure," she said. "At least until the bad guys chase you down."

"Good point," Cain said with a smile. He looked at her. "What are your plans?"

"I'll go home, have a hot shower, try to relax a little bit, and then figure out what to do with the rest of my five days off," she said.

"Perfect," Cain said. And his fingers tapped the table, almost as if he were impatient about something.

She looked at his fingers, looked at Cain, and shook her head. "Something is bothering you about me, but I don't know what."

Ryland reached across, grabbed her hand, and said, "Don't be defensive," he said. "Cain is wondering if you're in danger."

She stared at him, and her jaw dropped. "Danger?" she squeaked. "Why would I be in danger?"

"Because you rescued us, then you spent time with us. Since we're still alive, somebody may be worried about what we might have said to you."

"But what have you said to me?" she said. "It's not like I know anything."

"No, that's quite true," Cain said. "However, someone who may be worried about whether these guys survived would also be worried about what they know. Unfortunately, to the bad guys, you are now a loose thread. So they'll take care of you because, honestly, that's just what these guys do." Cain watched as Tabi retreated against her chair. "I'm sorry," he said. "I couldn't really do anything to make that part easier."

"It makes no sense," she said. "I'm the good guy here."

"So am I," Ryland said.

Cain snorted. "And me, if you want to go down that pathway. The problem with that line of thinking is that the bad guys don't care. They never do."

CHAPTER 6

TABI STARED AT the men in shock. "No, no, no," she said. "You have to be wrong. I was enjoying my holiday out on my boat and picked you up and took you to the naval ship. Nothing else there."

"By now, whoever tried to kill these men has already found out that these two are alive and that one was talking on a cell phone and that you went to visit him," Cain said. He shot her a direct look, his eyes more smoky gray than anything but ringed in thick dark lashes. "Didn't you?"

She frowned, slowly nodded, and said, "Of course I did. My phone was used to connect you two." Her gaze went back and forth from one to the other.

Cain nodded. "Exactly. So, whoever did this has already found out that you spent time with Ryland."

"But that doesn't mean Ryland was talking."

"No, but it does mean that the culprits have already connected with military personnel on that ship, and they already know that you two spent time together and contacted someone via cell phone."

"Does that mean somebody on the ship is bad?"

"Good and bad, it's a very hard distinction here," Cain said. "It could have been a simple question, passing in the mess hall or in the hallway. Whether the one guy survived, and would they make it? Somebody from the medical unit could have just mentioned in a conversation that one guy is up and talking, and the other one is not."

She sagged in her seat, as she stared at him, her mouth gaping. "Dear God," she said faintly. She stopped for a long moment, as she thought about it, and realized how it could be construed. "But doesn't that mean that everybody on that ship is in danger?"

"Possibly," he said, "but not likely. Doctors don't typically spend much time talking with patients. It would be whoever is back and forth, particularly in a scenario like this, because having rescued them, obviously you'll care about their future."

"Well, I cared about their immediate treatment."

"Also nobody can be sure whether you were injured or not," he said. "So that would be one of the other questions."

"Wow," she said. "I'm not sure I like the world you live in."

"You don't have to," he said. "But it is where we all live, and there's really no way around it."

"So how much danger are we talking about?"

He thought about it and shook his head. "The immediate danger is of more concern," he said. "I'll say it's probably a 60/40 chance."

"Wow," she said. "Not even 50/50?"

He gave her a lopsided grin. "I'm erring on the side of caution."

"Well, in that case, could you just make it 100 percent that I'm not in danger?"

"Well, I could," he said, "but is that really what you want to hear?"

"What I want," she said, "was for none of this to have happened."

"That's a given," he said. "I'd like to have Bullard here with us, giving us shit for talking to you about this at all. But that isn't exactly happening either."

At the reminder of their missing friend, she felt terrible. "Making me feel guilty because I'm not your missing friend won't help," she announced.

Ryland laughed. "I really do like the fact that you fight back," he said, chuckling.

She glared at him. "I wouldn't have been nice to you if I'd realized you would cause me this kind of headache," she snapped. But she didn't mean it. And, of course, he knew it. She groaned and said, "What am I supposed to do? I mean, I have five more days off, and then I return to work."

"I don't know that five days is enough," Cain said.

"It damn well better be," she said.

Ryland said, "Realistically it could take a couple weeks."

"I'm not taking a couple weeks off work," she snapped. "Unlike some people, I have to work a regular job for a living."

"We do too," Ryland said, with a smile. "It's just that our line of work ends up putting people into your line of work."

"That seriously sucks too," she said, "because my line of work is already swamped."

Both men gave clipped nods. But they didn't say anything more, and she studied them for a long moment.

"There's this odd sense of waiting that's around you," she said. Ryland looked at her in surprise. She shrugged. "It's as if you're waiting for something, and you're almost like a rubber band, pulled back as tight as it can go. Then, as soon as something happens, whatever it is you're waiting for," she said, with a wave of her hand, "you'll spring forth, like an arrow from a bow."

"That's not a bad analogy," Cain said. "We're waiting on news of Garret."

"What difference does it make?" she said. "He'll get his best care right here."

"And we're not leaving, until we know what his status is."

She understood that, at least partly. "As long as you don't think that your presence here will get him any better care."

Cain's lips twisted, as if there were something to that.

"We don't take people into emergency and sort them by whoever is waiting around outside," she said in a quiet tone.

"No, that's true," he said, "but the squeaky wheel does get the most care."

She frowned at that because she certainly had seen many doctors switch patients around just to get rid of somebody troublesome. "Sitting in the cafeteria is hardly being a squeaky wheel."

Ryland just chuckled. "Just wait until the doctor sees us when we go back."

She frowned at that and wondered. "Well, it's been almost an hour."

"Good enough," said Cain, as he stood.

She hadn't realized just how tall he was, until she was sitting here and he was standing. She slowly made her way vertical and said, "I would love to go home."

"Nothing is keeping you here," Ryland said. "If you want to go home now, you certainly don't have to wait on us."

"It's not a case of waiting on you, as much as it is trying to figure out if I'm safe," she muttered. "Did you mean to put the fear in me?"

"We meant for you to take extra care," Cain said.

"And how am I supposed to fight off someone who blew up a plane?" she asked.

"We don't expect you to," he said, "but we do expect you to take care with your personal safety."

"Taking care is a whole different story," she said. "I can take as many precautions as I want, and that necessarily won't improve anything."

"Understood, but, at the same time, maybe it will," he said. "If you notice anybody following you, looking at you suspiciously, hanging around—even when you walk into your apartment—if anybody's in a hallway, loitering, someone you don't know or don't recognize," he said, "you call us."

She frowned. "Call you on what? So far, Ryland has been using my phone."

At that, Ryland pulled a phone from his pocket.

She looked at it and said, "When did you get that?"

"Cain brought one for me," he said and held it so she saw his number.

She pulled hers out and quickly added it. "Fine," she said. "So I'll contact you. Then what?"

"Then we'll do something about it," Cain said smoothly.

She looked at him sharply, but a knowing smile was in his eyes. She shook her head. "Not likely. You'll be off doing whatever little revenge mission is on your mind."

"Not necessarily," Ryland said. "Obviously we're going back after answers. We need answers, and there's only one way to get them, but we won't forget you. You saved the both of us."

"Hardly saved," she said. "I just fished you out of the

water."

"Did you see any other boat around?" he asked. "Garret wouldn't have hung on too much longer."

"He was floating," she said. "You don't know how much longer he would have made it."

"I won't argue the point," Ryland said, his tone mild, "but we will look after you."

"Unless I get kidnapped on my way to the car," she snapped. She settled back and said, "Go on. Just do your thing. I'll grab a cab and go home."

"Or you could wait five minutes for us to check on Garret," Ryland said, as he stood. "I'll be a whole lot slower than Cain, and we have a rental that'll be here by the time we're done. Then we can drive you home. That way we can at least get the lay of the land and see how safe you are."

She hated to even understand the implications of what he suggested. "Do you think it's really necessary?" She knew she'd be a fool to not accept their help if they thought she was seriously in danger, but the whole thing really made no sense to her. "Isn't it a big stretch for anybody to consider me important in this fight you guys have going on?"

"I guess it depends on how big of a stretch *they* think it is, right?" Ryland replied. "If somebody had information you desperately wanted, and you could get it by grabbing them and knocking them around until they talked, what would you do?"

She frowned at him. "I hardly have any information that's important," she snapped.

"How will they know that until they knock you around a bit?"

She just glared at him and turned to head out of the cafeteria. Cain was a good six paces ahead of her, and Ryland was bringing up the rear. A position she realized was not an accident. She turned as they got to the doorway. "You're injured," she said. "You'll hardly be in a position to fight an attacker off."

"You'd be surprised," he said, his voice hardening. "When it comes to self-defense or self-preservation, we do all kinds of things that you don't think we can do."

RYLAND DIDN'T WANT to scare Tabi, but, at the same time, he didn't know exactly what was going on. It had only just occurred to him that she could be in danger. He thought about who knew how they'd survived and what they might have said. That had led him down a dangerous rabbit hole because it was one thing for her to be murdered, shot in cold blood, raising an investigation, but it was another thing entirely for her to die in "an accident." In that case, nobody would question anything, and she would become just another accident victim. That's something he couldn't live with.

She'd gone out of her way to keep him and Garret alive, and that was more important than anything. She'd already shown who and what she was on the inside, and he could do no less than help to support her now, knowing that things could get ugly. He didn't really want to fill her with fear, but she needed to be aware that some serious danger could be attached to her life at this point.

He wished she could take a month or two off work, but, of course, she needed to earn a living too. He pondered the problem as they walked back into the ER. Tabi walked in ahead of Ryland and Cain, and the doctor looked at her and smiled, but his gaze faltered when he saw the two men, and his friendly demeanor immediately stiffened into something much more formal.

"Results are back," he said. "Your friend will survive this. He's in a coma, and he'll wake up when he's ready. He's got significant bruising on the brain, and that'll just take some time to heal. Obviously he has several other medical issues that have all been attended to, and a few more that we'll keep an eye on, but we want to keep him here, under observation, rather than transferring him to another hospital."

Cain looked at him and nodded. "We're fine with that," he said. "Providing he gets the best care possible."

"That's a given, and I believe he'll recover," the doctor said quietly. "Unless anything new comes up."

At that, Ryland stepped forward and handed the doctor his card with a phone number on it. "Contact us with any change."

The doctor took the business card and nodded. "Will you guys be in town?"

"Somebody will be," Cain said, his voice hard. "It doesn't matter if we're right here or not. You can always contact us at that number." He walked to Garret's bedside and grabbed his buddy by the hand. Leaning over, he whispered something in his ear.

Ryland understood because his time would be next. He knew that the other two were watching Cain. When he straightened, looked down at his friend, his face getting harder with fury before he controlled every nuance on his face, he then turned and stepped back, facing Ryland.

Ryland walked up, gripped Garret's hand, and, leaning over the other side, said, "Buddy, we're here to look after you. You heal up while we go after the ones who did this. When I get back, I want to see you sitting up and laughing.

No other outcome is acceptable." He took a long look into the face of his friend, then turned and walked away. He looked at the doctor intently and said, "*Any* change."

The doctor nodded.

Ryland slung an arm around Tabi's shoulders. "Let's go."

"And if I don't want to?" she muttered. Her voice was low, so nobody but him heard it.

"Sweetheart," he replied, "we are well past being refused. That just won't work."

She looked at him, and he saw a change in her expression. An awareness of how her world had just shifted.

"Is this what happens when you do something nice for other people?" she asked, but no bitterness was in her voice, as if she were resigned to this ending.

"No," he said. "Not normally. But I for one really appreciate the fact that you did."

She shook her head. "I don't want to end up dead over this."

He squeezed her shoulders gently and tucked her closer to him. He rested his head against hers for a moment as they walked down the hallway behind Cain. "Listen. I will do my utmost best to make sure that doesn't happen."

CHAPTER 7

O UTSIDE, TABI WASN'T surprised to find a huge black truck, with a canopy in back and a double cab in the front, waiting for them. She sighed and said, "Of course you need something like this, don't you?"

"We do, yes," Ryland said. He helped her up into the front of the truck, and she watched as he got in behind her, showing absolutely no sign of being impeded by his injuries.

"You're not made of steel, you know?" she muttered.

"Nope, I'm not," he said. "But, by the same token, I know my limits."

She provided directions on how to get to her place and wasn't surprised when it was already up in the GPS. "You really are those supersecret spy kind of people, aren't you?" she said, with a resigned sigh.

"I don't know about that," Cain said quietly, "but what we do affects the security of millions of people."

She nodded and stared out the front windshield. It was weird for her to think that, in an hour, they would be gone from her life, and she'd be trying to get back to the normality of what she had prior to sailing on the ocean not a week earlier. In a boat lost at sea, which she had not yet allowed herself to grieve over. Of course many people would laugh at her and say it was foolish. It was just a piece of property, after all.

Maybe she would eventually feel mad because she'd lost something valuable, but it was the intangible value of the boat that she would grieve the loss of—where she had spent many wonderful hours with her younger brother. Hours in which she had worked to gain solace over losing him, when he lost the battle with leukemia. It had been her way of healing, after she had railed against the medical system and the lack of medical assistance available to him.

The medical world wasn't at fault; they just didn't have the technology to handle his particular strain. Some diseases, well, they were just terminal. And, of course, the moment you were born, death was a guarantee. It was a matter of when and how it came about that people tried to keep messing with.

She certainly hoped that Garret had many long and happy years ahead of him. She'd seen many a coma patient come back out of one after the doctors had given up hope. She'd also seen perfectly healthy men who had just dropped dead on the street. It was like fate picked a number, and it was your day. And that just depressed her even more. When they pulled up in front of her apartment complex, she looked at it and groaned. "Not exactly the five days left of my holiday I had planned."

"I'm sorry about that," Ryland said. "You're right. Being out sailing on that beautiful water is a whole different story, compared to sitting here."

"But I don't necessarily have to sit here either." She waited until Ryland hopped out; then she slipped out beside him. She turned to look at him, then Cain, as he joined them, and said, "You don't have to come up to my place. I'll be fine." Neither man listened to her, as they closed the doors and locked up the truck, then followed her to the front entrance of the apartment building. Knowing that it was futile to even argue, she headed up to her second-floor corner apartment, but his earlier words had stuck with her.

Even now, she looked at everybody and everything to see if anyone was watching her. She could almost feel a sense of being observed, but, for all she knew, it was because both men were with her, obviously watching out for her. As she got to her apartment, she quickly went to unlock the door and stopped in her tracks. Pushing open the already unlocked door, she froze.

Swearing softly, Ryland used his elbow to push the door forward. He stepped inside and turned to look back at her. "I presume you don't leave your place unlocked like this."

Her face blanched, and she shook her head, her hair flying wildly around her features. "Of course not," she said. "I haven't been here in what? Nine days? I think I flew out nine days ago." She stepped carefully inside behind him, with Cain coming in after her. She stared at her living room, which had been completely trashed. "Why would somebody do this?" she asked, her arms outstretched.

"It appears they came here, looking for you," Cain said.

"Well, I'm obviously not here," she snapped. "Why rip open the cushions?"

"Normally I'd say they were looking for something, but I'm not sure just what anybody would be looking for in this case."

"And why?" she said. "It's not like I've been here to stash some theoretical thing here connected to the airplane crash. Even if I was on the naval ship with the guys, or even on my sailboat for a time with Ryland and Garret, it's not like they gave me anything." She turned to face Ryland. "Surely you guys weren't looking for or carrying contraband of some sort, were you?" Then she immediately answered her own question. "And it doesn't even matter if you were, since you were blasted into the water, without warning."

"Exactly," he said. "No, we weren't carrying anything on board, and we didn't have anything when we got out of the water, as you well know."

She nodded. "Your clothes were torn up and halfway off you as it was," she said, as she walked a few steps forward and turned to look around. "I just don't get it," she said, as she surveyed the enormity of the mess the intruders had made. She walked into the kitchen and said, "Jesus! And this makes absolutely no sense either." All the pickles, relish, various mustards, and other condiments from the fridge had been taken out, upended, and dumped everywhere. "This isn't a normal robbery," she said. "This isn't somebody walking in and getting pissed off that I didn't have something in particular they were looking for. This is just deliberately making a mess." She looked at them. "But why?"

At that, Ryland frowned. "The only thing I can think of is, one, to make you leave. Two, to cause you all kinds of chaos and make you worried maybe. And three ..." He looked back at Cain and said, "I don't really have a three. Do you?"

"This is a deliberate act," Cain said. "But, other than to chase you away, I don't know why."

"And, if I were to be chased away," she said, looking at the two men, "where would I go anyway?"

Immediately both men spun around. "That *is* the question. Where would you go?"

She looked at them, puzzled, and said, "I don't understand."

"If this chased you away, where would you go?"

She frowned and thought about it. "I don't know," she said. "I have friends I could bunk with overnight, I guess. My friend's boat may be here—the one I can use when I've got some free time. If I could contact her and make sure the boat is in her slip, and she doesn't have other plans for it, I could go to the marina and sleep on it overnight. I'd probably just end up in a hotel, frustrated and angry, trying to get insurance to fix this up," she said.

"Would you call the cops?"

"Sure, I would," she said. "This is obviously breaking and entering, but it's more vandalism than anything else."

"Nuisance value."

"Yes," she said. "But there's got to be a message behind it." She walked to the master bedroom, and her heart sank. All her bedding, all the clothes from the closet and drawers were all dumped and tossed around. She walked into the bathroom and saw something on the mirror and stared. "Well, I found the message," she called out. Both men followed her into the bathroom, and she pointed to the lipstick message on the glass.

Bitch, we're on to you!

She looked at the men. "But *on to me* about what?"

Cain spoke first. "Is there any other reason, something completely unrelated to Ryland here, that would cause you to believe somebody was doing this on a personal level?"

"You mean, like some ex-boyfriend or a really upset girl-friend, coworker?" she asked.

"Anything," Ryland said. "Personal relationships, work, family, neighbors."

"No," she said, crossing her arms over her chest. "And I really hate to think that you guys will start digging into my background."

"Are you hiding anything?" Ryland asked bluntly. "This is really not the time or place to be trying to hide something from us."

"I'm not hiding anything. My life has been fairly simple up until now. I don't have anything to hide. My last relationship was about five months ago, and we broke it off peaceably."

"Is there such a thing?" Cain asked her curiously.

"Well, let's just say I suspected that he was screwing around on me, and I didn't wait to find out for sure. I didn't care to be with him anymore, so I just told him that we were done," she said. "He agreed and said it wasn't working out for him either, and we split. Easy," she said.

"Why did you end up taking this holiday alone?" Cain asked.

She looked up at them in surprise. "Let me guess. Do you think that a woman can't do anything without a man nearby?"

Ryland immediately held up his hand. "No, we're not going there at all. What we're getting at is why you chose this time and place for your holiday."

"Because it commemorates the death of my brother, who my boat was named after," she snapped in frustration and tears. "He died of leukemia six years ago. So, every year, I take time off from work, and I go sailing. All of the medical staff at the hospital know. It's my way to get back in touch with what really matters in life."

At that, a moment of silence came from the other two. "So pretty much anybody at the hospital would have known you were out there on the boat?" Cain asked.

"Yes." She raised her hands in frustration. "Surely you don't think your plane was blown up in that exact spot, at that exact time, all so I would find you?" she sneered. "Even the gods couldn't have made that happen."

"No," he said, "but obviously they would have known your place was empty."

She thought about it and nodded. "Yes, as well as several of my neighbors here and anybody I worked with. Not to mention others, like the newspaper boy, and probably a half-dozen more I've mentioned it to. I've lived here a long time, so I know people. I'm social with them to a certain extent, and I would expect a certain amount of social small talk at various times. So, yes, people would know, but we can hardly go blame everybody who would know."

"No, but it just means that there was an opportunity and a motive, and somebody took it."

"So, we're back to thinking that this is related to Ryland and that they got here before I got back?"

"As soon as you were picked up by the naval ship, the bad guys knew that you would be home within a day or two, so they probably came in yesterday," Cain said. "Listen. If you have insurance, they'll cover this, but obviously you can't stay here."

"Well, I could," she said, as she looked around. "It would take a long time to clean up this mess, but the bedroom is still serviceable. I could toss everything, go buy a quick change of sheets, and sit in my room, while I await the insurance adjuster, and then get this place cleaned up. But it wouldn't be pleasant, right?" She looked back to see them staring at each other, their gazes hard. "What are you thinking?"

"You're coming with us," Ryland said.

"Like hell I am," she said. "No way you'll convince me that, if I'm not with you, I'll be in more trouble, and, if I'm with you, I'll be better off."

"But you will be," he said. "It'll be obvious to anybody who's watching you that you're not alone and that you're not helpless in this world."

"Gosh, I can't remember the last time I was helpless," she said coolly, leaning against the now-closed refrigerator door. She looked around at her apartment and said, "You know what? I won't cry out of frustration for something like this, but it does make me angry as hell." She looked at them. "So, if you have all these superspy bullshit skills, can you check into the cameras for the apartment, and see who did this?"

Cain gave her a smile, while Ryland looked at her with a chuckle. "It's already happening," he said. "We should have an answer pretty quick."

Just then Cain's phone buzzed. He pulled it out, read the text, and said, "Single male, five-ten, with lighter skin and freckles, but his face was kept away from the cameras. He wore a hat down low and a sports jacket over jeans and sneakers."

She snorted at that. "You got a photo already?"

He tapped away on the phone for a moment, and, when it buzzed again, he held it up. "Do you recognize this person?"

She looked at an image of what could have been nearly anybody. She sighed and said, "No. So how did he get in?"

"A key apparently. But busted up the door for good measure."

"Great," she said. "So one guy did all of this? He must have been here for what—an hour, two hours?"

"Two hours and twenty-two minutes," Cain said, reading the text. "He left the same way. He was picked up on the outside of the parking lot on foot."

"And I guess, if he'd parked nearby, we would have gotten a vehicle model and license plate."

"Yeah, and we'd have tracked him into the city as well," Ryland said.

"So what does this make him?"

The two men looked at each other, looked back at her, and Cain said, "A pro."

THAT WAS A concern in itself. But it fell along the lines of somebody coming after him and Garrett. More likely Bullard, and any of his team that they could take out, these pros would take out.

Ryland looked back at Cain. "Was anybody on the Australian team attacked?"

Cain gave him a sharp glance and said, "Interesting you'd ask that. You know how we switch vehicles out of instinct? We did that on our way back. And the vehicle we'd been renting blew up on the highway."

Ryland just stared at him. "So this attack isn't just about going after Bullard. They're after all of us."

"That's what I'm starting to think," he said, with a wave of his arm toward Tabi. "Apparently casualties don't matter."

"Shit," Ryland said. "Did we get any updates on all the suspects being run down?"

"Out of the nineteen that we narrowed it down as maybe possible, they've knocked six off the list."

"I remember you talking about that," Tabi said, stepping closer. "How do you know those six are off the list?"

"Five are dead, one's in a coma," he said.

"Okay," she said, shoving her hands in her pockets. "I

guess they're off the list. And the others?"

"Nothing yet," he said.

"What about family and friends of those six?" Tabi asked.

Cain nodded. "Checking those too."

She looked around and said, "Okay. I'll grab a bag of clothes and get out of here. Then I need to go sit at a coffee shop or somewhere and make some phone calls."

"What about your electronics?" Ryland looked at her.

"Well, I have a laptop here, somewhere."

"Maybe," he said. "That's something you need to find."

She walked into her bedroom, grabbed a carry bag from the closet, one of the few things still sitting on the floor. She sorted through some of the clothes, looking for what she could use. She was just desperate enough that she would have to recycle most of what hadn't been damaged too badly, although it looked like her intruder had taken a knife to a lot of things. By the time the men stepped into the bedroom, she had a bag of bits and pieces.

"We can't find the laptop."

She looked up at them, frowned, and said, "Did you check under the coffee table? There's a little space, and I often just park it under there."

Ryland disappeared from view.

"We checked everywhere else," Cain said. He looked at the small bag. "Is anything salvageable here?"

"Not much," she said. "Pretty much everything here has been cut up or sliced. I've got a couple changes of clothes, not necessarily in the shape I'd like them to be, but I'll take what I can get just now. Even the bedding was slashed and so is the mattress."

"I'll take pictures," Cain said, starting now with her bedroom. "Get whatever you want and also check the bathroom for anything too. Make sure you check the drawers. Then we'll do a complete sweep of photographs, so you'll have them for the insurance."

Just then Ryland came back, sporting a big grin on his face. "It was completely hidden, just like you said. So, even when he dumped over the table, he didn't see it." He held up the laptop and a charger cord.

"Perfect," she said. "I need to salvage something out of this mess." She opened it and pushed the power button. When it fired up, she grinned, shut it off again, and packed it in her bag. She grabbed her bag and headed out to the living room. Cain followed, still taking photos.

"Did you want to look and see if you can find the mouse to go with that?"

"Looking for it still," Tabi said.

"We need to widen our circle of suspects," Ryland said to Cain. "If they're supposedly after just Bullard, why would they go after the team?"

"That's easy," Tabi said with spirit. "To make sure the team didn't go after them."

Both men nodded.

"Are you ready to leave?" Cain asked. "I've got photos of every room for your insurance company."

"Sure," she said, looking around and spotting her mouse on top of a heap on the floor. "There. That's the last thing I needed." She snatched it up and tucked it into her bag.

"Are you sure you don't need anything else?"

"I don't think so," she said. "I'll have to come back with the insurance agent, I'm sure."

"Yeah," Ryland said. "Just make sure nothing is left here that may be important."

"Where are we going?"

"We've got a hotel," he said. "You can make your phone calls from there."

"Fine," she muttered. "But there's got to be other stuff I can do to get my life back on track."

"You can help us," Ryland said.

As they walked out, she turned to lock the door and then shook her head, as it didn't even lock anymore. "Since they got in so easily, why did they feel the need to break it all up?" she asked. And once again Cain took photos, and they just closed the door as best they could and headed down to the vehicle. "I'm notifying the landlord to at least fix the lock."

"Is there any chance that somebody is watching us now?" she asked a bit nervously.

"Guaranteed," Ryland said. "They'll know by now that I'm alive and that Cain is here with me."

"So how do you know that, while we were in there, they didn't put something on the truck?"

Ryland looked at her and smiled, as he said, "We don't."

Cain was ahead of her. As they got to the truck, Ryland grabbed her arm and held her back slightly. "That's exactly what he's checking for right now." As she watched, Cain pulled something from his pocket, turned it on, and ran it slowly around the vehicle.

"What's he looking for?"

"Electronics that don't belong," Ryland said. "Like detonators or a cell phone, remote-access bombs."

"What about good old-fashioned pipe bombs or even C-4?"

"We'll get there," he said, and, as she watched, Cain ducked underneath and checked the undercarriage of the truck. He walked all the way around and opened the vehicle.

"If he opened up that door, he could have blown up too."

"That's what the little machine in his hand is doing," Ryland said.

"I get it," she said, "but aren't we relying on technology too much?"

"Have you got something against technology?" he asked, laughing.

Cain gave him the all clear, and Ryland nudged her forward and said, "Let's go." Inside the vehicle, all three of them sharing the roomy front seat, Cain started up the engine. Only as they pulled away could Ryland feel her relaxing. "Did you really think it would blow up when we drove out?"

"It felt like a distinct possibility," she muttered. She linked her hands nervously in front of her, and he reached across, separated them, and loosely laced his beat-up fingers with hers. She looked down at his swollen hand. "You should be in bed," she said. "You shouldn't even be out here, dealing with this crap."

"Well, somebody has a different idea," he said.

"I get it," she replied, "but it doesn't make any sense."

"Bullard made a lot of enemies," Cain said, beside her. "We just have to narrow it down to which one it is."

"Is it that easy?" she asked.

"No," he said. "It's not easy at all. Somebody went to great lengths to send us off in different directions on wild goose chases, leaving red herrings, to make sure they aren't caught."

"So how will you figure it out?"

"We'll chase down every thread we can and, with any luck, start finding pieces of the puzzle. Eventually we'll have all those pieces."

"That could take months," she said, her skin pale.

"It could," he said. "But, hey, it's not like we have anything more important to do."

CHAPTER 8

T ABI WASN'T THAT surprised when they ended up in a building that she wouldn't even have recognized as a hotel. "How do you know this is even a hotel?" she asked. "There's no big name, no doorman, no reception area, nothing."

"It's on the private side," Ryland murmured against her ear, as he nudged her forward.

"More secret superspy stuff, huh?"

"Maybe," he said cheerfully.

She looked at him and saw the tinge of pain on his face. "You need your antibiotics and pain pills."

"And I need food," he said, with a smile.

"I don't think they'll have a dining room here," she said.

"Nope, but we can order in, anything we want."

"What, like fast food?"

"Sure, if that's what you'd like?"

She shrugged. "I guess pizza or something, if nothing else works."

"Well, we could get a steak too, if we want," he said.

She smiled. "How about steak and lobster?"

"If you want it," he said. "Definitely."

She shrugged. "I'd rather have a big plate of spaghetti and meatballs."

"Excellent," he said. He loved the way she thought and

how quickly her mind worked. "Agreed," he said, as they walked down a hallway. "So this isn't just about Bullard either, by the way. We have a lot of different guys who we have to go after now, in order to figure out what's going on. But we'll get there, I promise," he added, as he showed her into the room.

When she saw the single room with two beds, she shook her head. "You guys don't have room for me here."

"Yes, we do," Cain said. "As long as you're willing to share."

She shrugged. "I'm so damn tired, I don't even care anymore," she said, as she tossed her bag on the floor next to the nearest bed and crashed down on half of it. "I want to know what we're supposed to do from here though."

"We'll order food, and you'll call your insurance company," Ryland said.

Cain added, "I'll grab a shower. It's been a bloody long night."

"Good idea," Ryland replied, as Cain turned and walked into the bathroom.

Ryland walked to the small table against the window and said, "Go ahead and make your calls before you crash."

She frowned, looked at him, and said, "What made you so bossy?"

He chuckled. "Life."

When he brought out his own laptop, she looked at it and said, "Where'd you get that?"

"Cain brought it for me."

"Of course. I should have known. So, how long have you known Cain?"

"A dozen years," he said, looking over the top of the laptop. "Why?"

"Just wondering," she said. "Looks like he was there for you and anticipated what you would need."

"That's the way our team works," he said.

She nodded, smiled, and said, "You're lucky."

"I don't know about luck," he said. "It's a give-and-take deal, and it's hard work."

"I know," she said sadly. "My brother was really important to me, and, since losing him, ... since then, I've just kept myself ... isolated, I guess."

"You'd probably started to isolate yourself. Before you had friends, but then your brother needed more care, more support, so some of your friends drifted away. Then, by the time he was gone, you turned around and realized you were alone."

"That's about right," she said, sitting up and looking at him. "I guess you've seen it happen before, huh?"

"Many times," he said. "Because of the work we do, we sometimes see people in the worst situations imaginable, and we hear all kinds of stories. None of it's easy, on anybody."

"No," she said, then got up off the bed, walked to the table, and sat across from Ryland. "I think you should take a few days off," she said earnestly.

He shook his head. "No more days off for me. We have to work as fast as we can now. The fact is, the team has already been working on this in the background, but I'll need to do some legwork pretty fast."

"Do you think the bad guys followed us here?"

"Yes, and regardless of whether they're trying to take out the team and Bullard—or take out Bullard and see what the team knows—Cain and I are targets."

"Which makes me a target as well, just because I'm with you," she announced. "How was that better than me staying at my apartment?"

"Well, your apartment was already targeted," he said. "Do you think they won't go back and see if you're home?" He smiled. "You're still better off here with us, where you've got some protection, than at home alone, where they could pick you up at any time and try to use you against us."

She stared at him. "Are you serious? Would they do that?"

"If they could, yes," he said simply. "Of course I would come and try to save you, as you saved me. And, if somebody would have taken you off the street and used you as bait, I'd definitely fall for it. But I would come with a team."

"Which they would expect."

He nodded. "They would, so it would end up being who was the smartest, fastest, and best shot."

"Which would really suck because there'd be deaths on both sides."

"They don't calculate that because they just hire cheap local gunmen," he said. "In which case, whoever it is won't care about his team and would be happy to have them all go down—fewer witnesses."

"God," she said, as she stood, spun around, and leaned against the wall. "This is mind-bending. Just a couple days ago, I was lying around on my boat, enjoying being out on the water."

"Were you really? Or were you wondering what you'll do with your life now?" he asked.

Startled, she looked at him.

He shrugged and said, "I just wondered."

"Yeah, I was doing some of that," she admitted. "Life tends to get in a bit of a rut after a while."

"It does, indeed," he said. "When you think about it, an

awful lot is going on in your world. And it's not all bad."

"It's not bad at all," she said, "but I'm not exactly getting anywhere."

"You're totally getting somewhere."

"Says you," she muttered.

"I wish you could just deal with the day in front of you," he said.

"Maybe, but at the same time, everything feels unfinished somehow."

"And I think that would probably be normal," he said.

"Maybe. I just want this all to be over with now."

"You and me both," he said, as he started tapping away, obviously focusing on what was in front of him.

She grabbed her phone, pulled up the last email she had from the insurance broker, and found the phone number. Quickly she called them. When she got someone she had dealt with for a few years, she was relieved.

"Hey, Sandy," she said. "I was away on holiday, and I'm back now, but, while I was gone, my apartment was broken into, and vandals just went through and trashed everything." She listened as the woman on the other end exhaled in dismay. "I know. I need to call the police, don't I?" With that confirmed, she pulled out a piece of paper and jotted down notes. "Okay, if you want to open a file, I'll have the cops come by and take a look and open up a case on it. A threat was on the mirror too, but I think it was probably just kids."

She listened as Sandy rattled off what they would do about it. First, they would contact the insurance company who'd given her coverage and confirm the next step, having an adjuster out to see the property and the scene of the crime. The yacht was a different company but she'd contact them as well.

After the local police saw the crime scene as well, then she would have the apartment cleared out, and they would reimburse her, based on whatever her coverage was, for the furniture and personal goods. Thankfully she did have renter's insurance, and, if any damage was done to the actual building, that would have to be taken care of by the building owner and management, under their own insurance policy.

"Thank you very much, Sandy," she said, relieved she did have $25,000 coverage for personal belongings, which wasn't a ton when she considered her electronics alone, but she would replace everything anyway. She had been given the chance to raise her coverage a while back and had done so. Good thing.

While she was at it, she went ahead and called the cops. She explained that she'd contacted the insurance company and been told that she had to contact the police about the break-in. By the time she had that dealt with that, she had agreed to call her apartment manager to let the cops in to see the crime scene tomorrow morning at nine a.m.

She hung up the phone and asked, "Did you order food?"

"Huh?" he answered, his voice distracted.

She glared at him. "Cain'll be out of the shower any minute, and there's no food."

This time he lifted his gaze and said, "I ordered it."

She sagged in a chair and nodded. "Okay. Did you find out anything interesting?"

"Yes," he said. "On one of our cases about a year ago, we went in after some kidnap victims. We rescued all but one, a young girl we found, already dead. We carried her out of there, but obviously we couldn't save her because she had died before we got there."

"Ouch," she said. "What about it?"

"The father was beside himself, and he blamed us."

"Why?"

"We didn't get there in time, as far as he was concerned, and potentially that was part of it. I mean, if we could have gotten there a day earlier, maybe she would have been alive, but there's no way to know. And we never found out why or how she died. So we don't know if that timing would have made a difference or not."

"And you think the father is behind this?"

"Instinct is telling me it's somewhere around him. All attempts to find him have failed."

"Meaning?"

"Meaning, he's gone underground."

"Well, that's possible," she said. "I mean, if he'll put something like this in motion, he doesn't want to be someplace where he could get easily found and caught."

"Exactly," he said.

"Any family, friends, or anybody like that who you could talk to?"

"We actually worked with two of his men on another job after that. They were the ones who told us how upset the father still was."

"Why were you working with them?"

"We needed a couple more guys, and Bullard gave them both a try. They were looking for more work, and they were under contract to the father but potentially were looking to move."

"What happened to them?"

"They both went back to work with the father," he said, sitting back. "And now that I think about it, since they went back, all they did was gather intel from us."

"Meaning, they were working for the father all along?"

"That's what I would expect, yes," he said, frowning.

"So you expect those two men came after us?"

"Maybe," he said. "Though that seems very simple."

"What about this father? Did he have the means to do all this and the know-how?"

"Not necessarily. But he's connected to some very big Saudis in the oil industry."

"Well, they definitely have the clout and some big money," she said, surprised. "But would they really care?"

"And that's always the problem, isn't it?"

"Maybe that's just what they want you to think, because of the timing."

"Maybe." He grabbed the notepad beside him and wrote down names and dates.

"Is this all about the same father?"

"And another case," he said, "which just might dovetail. I'm not sure."

She gave him some time and space. So she searched the web on her phone, then checked her emails, basically looking for anything to keep her mind occupied, while she tried to figure out what she would do now. When a knock came on the door, she froze and looked at him.

He'd already stood, heading toward the door. When he got to the door, he made an odd sound. Another odd sound came from the other side. Immediately he opened the door, and a big cart was pushed in. She looked at him in surprise. The guy never said a word, then turned and walked back out again. As soon as he was gone, Ryland walked to the bathroom door and called out to Cain, "Food's here."

"I'm done," Cain said, as he opened the door and

stepped out. His hair was wet, and he was obviously clean-shaven. He looked like he felt better, at least for the moment. He smiled when he saw the trolley. "Good," he said. "Let's see if we can clear some space."

There were only two chairs, so she said, "I can sit on the bed."

"We'll see," he said, as they lifted the lids. Indeed, there was a steak for each man, but when the third dome came off, she laughed to see spaghetti and meatballs. He held it out to her with a fork, and she smiled in joy.

"You were serious, weren't you?" she said.

"Never more so," he said. "I told you that you can have pretty well anything."

She rearranged the pillows and scooched up against the headboard. She sat with her plate of spaghetti on her lap. It was piping hot and delicious. It was so good. She could only eat slowly because it was so hot, whereas the men attacked their meals with vigor. She said to Cain, "Ryland's wondering about a couple cases."

Cain looked at Ryland, who shrugged and said, "Just thinking about that job we did in South Africa. You know? For the father whose daughter died?"

"I wondered about him too," Cain said. "Although that's almost, like, too easy."

"I know. I was thinking that too. It's, like, he's the obvious culprit that we'll think about immediately," Ryland said. "But then there was that other one," Ryland said, as he tapped the notepad. "I was wondering if they dovetailed together somehow."

"That was a friend of his, wasn't it?"

"Yes. And remember? We had two of the father's henchmen come and work for us. Then they went back and worked for him again afterward."

"Meaning, that maybe they were still working for the father the whole time they were working for you," she suggested curiously.

"Yeah, that's something that came up in one of our meetings."

"You haven't had time for any meetings," she said in exasperation.

"We have meetings constantly on the phone or the laptop," he said. "We're going through as many files as we can, trying to see who would bear that kind of a grudge."

"Or multiple grudges," she said. "Maybe it's somebody who just had a small grudge but figures that other people have been slighted or wronged, and you need to be taken out collectively."

"That's pretty big thinking," Cain said. "I can't imagine it. I suspect this is a very small, fairly intimate group."

"Blowing up a plane," she snapped, "is not intimate. Watching somebody die as you strangle the life out of them? *That's* intimate."

Both men looked at her in surprise.

"I'm a surgical nurse. Remember? I've seen plenty of what people do to each other," she said. "There's a lot of differences in the way people kill and maim those who they supposedly love."

"That's very true," Cain said. "Well, at least now we might have something to go on."

"What's that?" she asked.

"We took a photo of the message in your bathroom. We looked at the handwriting, and one of the guys recognized something. Along with the photo we have from the video camera, we've narrowed down your intruder. It looks like it's a local merchant whose services are widely for sale," he said. "We'll have a talk with him tonight."

"Good," she said. "Let's hope he has something to offer."

Ryland looked at her and gave her a wolfish smile and said, "He will."

She glared at him. "You guys going to torture him for what he knows?"

"If need be, yes," Cain said smoothly. "What would you like us to do? Give him a key to your next place of residence?"

"Understood." She buried her fork in the spaghetti, eating, as she pondered what this next stage of her life would mean. She'd always been nonviolent, believing in peace, but what do you do when the war comes to your front doorstep? Do you fight back? Or did you let the war run over you? Because she didn't see that she had a whole lot of choice at this point. Apparently she was in this do-or-die scenario, and choices had to be made, but they needed to be made at once.

When she was done with her spaghetti, she returned her plate to the cart, looking to see that the men were all done too. She removed their plates and stacked them all up.

"Wait. What's the rest of this under here?" She lifted it up, found an apple pie and several small plates. "Are you kidding?" she said. "Not slices of pie, but a whole pie."

"Pie makes me think," Ryland said, with a laugh.

Cain looked at the trolley and said, "Bet there's coffee underneath too."

She lifted the white tablecloth that went over the trolley surface and, sure enough, found a coffee service underneath. She poured coffee for everyone and cut the pie. She took a good-size piece for herself, as the men came over to help themselves, and she watched as they took a full one-quarter each. She was left gasping at the amount. "You can't be hungry, surely?"

"There's always room for pie," they said, nearly in unison. Just then both of their phones buzzed, and both men immediately snatched theirs up.

Cain looked at his and frowned, then said, "Ice, what's up?"

Tabi lost track of his response, distracted when she heard Ryland, saying, "Dr. Stevenson, what's up?"

He got up and walked toward her to move away from Cain's conversation. "What kind of change?" He frowned at her and asked the doc, "Is it serious?" He paused. "Right, okay." When he hung up, he frowned and said, "So they've decided to go in and relieve some pressure on the brain after all," he said. "Is that good or bad?"

"Both," she said. "Bad, in the sense that they feel the pressure is building inside the skull to the point that they need to do something about it, and good that they're going in to do it. Because that will hopefully stop any brain damage, helping Garret to recover faster."

"Okay," Ryland said, relief crossing his face.

She smiled. "They are looking after him, you know?"

"They better be."

JUST SEEING DR. Stevenson's name on his phone had been enough to make Ryland's heart slam against his chest. If anything happened to Garret, Ryland didn't know what he would do. Garret was the younger of them, the one Ryland had taken under his wing. He felt half responsible for him, even though he had turned out to be a hell of a man all on his own. And he was an equal partner in all this. Garret would also be damn pissed to hear Ryland making any comments that made him sound like he was somehow less than others on the team. But Garret was a good guy, and to have this happening to him was just shitty.

As Ryland sat here thinking of Garret, he flashed on something he had seen back in Texas. He focused on it, trying to bring the memory closer, but it wouldn't come. He thought something was there, somebody talking to Bullard before they got on the plane at Houston. Who the hell was that? He frowned, reached for his phone, and called Eton. "Hey, can you backtrack to the cameras of the Houston airport? My brain's a little on the wonky side still, and my memories aren't all filled in yet, but I have a vision of Bullard talking to somebody on the tarmac before we took off. I don't remember much, but it was just that sense of somebody being there."

"The camera feeds are really terrible," Eton said, "but we'll give it a go."

"Do that," Ryland said and hung up the phone. He found himself still trying to pull the memory forward, when Cain put his phone down. Ryland turned to look at Cain.

"The meeting is set for an hour from now."

"Meeting?" she asked.

Cain smiled. "Let's just say, our local merchant for sale, he'll be at his favorite pub tonight, so we'll find him there."

"Great, where will we take him on?" Ryland asked.

"How about the back alleyway?" Cain said, with a laugh.

"If it's private, then yes," he said. "Otherwise we could pick him up at home."

"Maybe," he said. "Depends on if he shows up at the pub on time or not."

Tabi looked into her coffee and then back at the men. "Am I coming?"

Both turned and said, "No."

Nodding, she settled back and said, "Good. In that case I'll watch some TV. I hope you don't mind." She grabbed the remote and turned it on. The two men looked at each other, smiled, and sat back down. Ryland knew what she was doing; she was trying to forget about everything that was going on and about the upcoming meeting. In this case, the term *meeting* was a bit of a euphemism. What they really planned to do was ambush and isolate the man and have a little talk with him. A very serious talk. They needed answers fast.

Ryland returned to his search on the laptop, just as a chat box opened up with Eton on the other side.

Here's the Houston video feeds, he wrote. **Take a look and tell us what you're looking for.**

Ryland quickly went through it, trying to bring it back to where he had approached the plane. He'd gotten on earlier with Garret, and Bullard had come on behind them. Ryland remembered hearing voices, but he couldn't see anybody. He looked and watched the video, but nothing was recognizable. He saw just the heads from the back on this feed. **Any cameras on the other side?**

Eton replied, **No cameras on the other side, so this is all we've got.**

I can hear the voices in my head and was thinking that something was slightly familiar about it but never could place it with all the surrounding noise. It could be my imagination. Looking for something where there's nothing.

Well, Ryland, a little more info would help, he wrote. **We're running out of time.**

I know. But it's back in Houston, so check the other camera feeds. We're looking for somebody we already know.

We're on it, he typed. **It's just hard to look for something in the middle of nothing.**

I know. I get it, Ryland wrote. **I'll let you know if anything rings a bell.** And he closed the chat box.

Cain stared at him. "Somebody Bullard was talking to?"

"Yes, I was inside the plane, talking with Garret, as we were waiting for Bullard," he said. "Then it occurred to me that he was out there, talking to somebody. I thought it was just small-talk, you know? Thanking the ground crew or something, but I remember thinking, something was very familiar about that voice."

"What'll it take to bring that forward?"

"I have no clue," he said, "Quite possibly nothing. I hate to say it but it wasn't clear enough to do anything with at this point."

CHAPTER 9

"WHILE YOU'RE OUT tonight," Tabi said, in a sarcastic tone, "why don't you just make sure to get hit over the head again?" He shot her a sharp look, and she shrugged her shoulders at him. "What? How do you expect your brain to heal when you haven't given it a chance? It's not like you're giving it any time or rest for that matter. Look at you. You have more fractures and stitches in you than most of the surgical patients in the hospital ... combined."

"I don't have time," he said.

"I get that," she said, softening her tone a little. "So have a little understanding when your body needs a little bit of time to bring back certain memories."

He grimaced at her, as he stood, then looked at Cain. "You ready?"

Cain stepped away from the table, snagged his jacket from the back of his chair, and slipped it on. "Absolutely."

As the two men walked toward the door, she felt something inside her shrinking. It was one thing to be here with them; it was another thing entirely to be alone. "How long will you be?" she asked, trying desperately to keep her voice on an even keel, but it didn't work.

Ryland walked back to her, reached down, and gave her a quick hug and a kiss on the forehead, as if something more were between them than actually was. "We'll be fine."

She nodded, and her bottom lip trembled. Then he hooked her chin with his finger and gave her a hard kiss. "Honest, we'll be fine."

"Sure you will," she said. "Your plane got blown up, and we all nearly drowned, and my place got destroyed, and, for the last twenty-four hours, we've been all over the planet."

"Yeah, but look how far we've come," he said with a chuckle. "You've got my number in your phone."

"I do. However, I won't call you, if you're in the middle of interrogating somebody with your fists."

"I'd appreciate it if you didn't call us right away anyhow," Cain said, from the doorway. "We don't want our phones to alert anyone that we're there."

"Great," she said. "So how do I order, like, a pot of tea and a cookie or something to make me feel better?"

"Comfort eating?" Ryland asked.

"If it works," she said with a sniff.

"We'll order you up something as we leave," he said. He turned and looked at her and said, "Don't wait up for us. If you're tired, you just need to sleep." And, with that, he walked out.

His last remark enraged her. "Like I could sleep now," she snapped. "How is that even possible?"

It's one thing, if they were all flopped here, and she could have the peace and comfort of knowing that she wasn't alone. But, as soon as that door closed, there was something insanely silent about the large space she was in. In a matter of moments, everything—the entire predicament of her world—all came crashing in on her. She was sharing a room in an unknown hotel—that didn't even look like a hotel—with two men who didn't look like they were normal average citizens either.

And now they were off on some secret mission to interrogate a potential suspect, and she didn't even want to know the details of what that meant. Her beloved boat was gone; she'd been rescued and brought in on a navy destroyer or some such ship, and here she was, with another four or five days left of her holiday. Some vacation.

As she sat here, mulling over the changes in her circumstances, she felt a chill encroaching. Grabbing a blanket from the bottom of the bed, she wrapped it around her shoulders and flipped through the TV channels aimlessly, looking for something to distract her, anything. About ten minutes later, a knock came on the door.

She froze, got up cautiously, and called out, "Yes?"

"We have tea for you. I'll leave it outside the door, as requested."

"Thank you."

She was at the door, her ear against it, but she didn't hear any sounds. She hesitated to open it, but the men had ordered her tea, and, damn it, she really wanted a hot cup. But then, was it anything more than a carrot, dangling in front of her, that made people make the stupidest mistakes? Still, she was supposed to be safe here, and she had to put her trust in the men. If she couldn't trust them, who could she trust?

She opened the door, and, sure enough, a much smaller trolley was here than last time, but definitely a trolley heaped with something. She poked her head down the hallway and took a look around but saw no sign of anyone. She pulled the trolley in, then quickly closed and locked the door. Lifting the lids, she smiled to see a selection of tea cakes on one serving dish and, on the other one, an array of cheese and crackers.

"Oh, yum," she said, as she pushed the cart toward her bed in delight. On the second shelf, she found a silver tea service, one of the long-handled, long-spouted things that she'd often seen at high-end restaurants but had never actually had for herself. Also fresh milk, lemon, and honey. Well, she only liked milk in her tea, but she appreciated the options. She crawled back onto the bed, wrapped herself up, and, with the trolley right beside her, poured herself a cup of tea. Then studied the plate of confections, everything from little tea cakes to meringues to even pieces of pie and cake, but everything was small. The trouble was, if the men would be gone for hours, chances are, she'd eat everything on the plate. Then again, weight wasn't an issue for her, and, right now, anything she could do to make herself feel better was good with her.

She chose one tea cake, put it on a smaller plate, and settled against the headboard to watch a good mystery. Just as she finished the first show in the series, she looked down at her watch to realize her attention has been captured for the whole forty-five minutes. As she studied her phone, it buzzed, and then it rang. It was her girlfriend from Sydney, who was holding the rest of her clothes for her. "Hello, Maureen. How are you doing?"

"More to the point, how are you doing?" she asked.

"I'm fine."

"Are you sure?" There was an odd note in her voice.

"Sure. Why?"

"I have a confession to make," Maureen said. "After you crashed the boat and were picked up by the navy ship and everything, I was out at the bar, and some guy, well, I let him pick me up, and I spent the night with him at a hotel."

"Which isn't really unusual for you, so why the confession?"

"No, what I didn't realize until later was that he was asking a lot of questions, about my friends, where I used to work, things like that. And I ended up telling him about you. He got really interested in what had happened, so I was explaining how you were a nurse in Perth and all ..." Her voice trailed off.

"And you think this is important, why?" Tabi asked.

"You're okay, right?" Maureen said hurriedly. "He didn't like come and do anything to you, right?"

"Why would you think that?"

"Well, we'd made plans for breakfast this morning. I was still on a bit of a high overnight and didn't notice, but, when I got up and went downstairs, expecting to meet him for breakfast, he didn't show up. I waited for an hour, and, when I asked after him at the reception desk, he had checked out late last night. So he did it deliberately," she said in outrage.

"Interesting," Tabi murmured.

"What does that mean?"

"My apartment was trashed," she said. "We're trying to figure out how anybody would know where I lived, and why someone would want to do that."

"Trashed?" Maureen's voice rose superhigh over the phone. "How bad?"

"Well, they tossed the furniture, threw the food all over everything, tore up all my clothing, at least the bulk of it was either slashed or torn," she said. "I'm supposed to meet the cops there tomorrow, and the insurance company has already been contacted. A message was on the bathroom mirror," she quickly explained. "So we're waiting on the police."

"Do you think he targeted me?" Maureen asked in horror.

"The only reason he would do that," Tabi said, "is if he knew about us being friends, but I don't know why he'd care."

"Sure, but lots of people know about us," she said. "Not to mention the fact that we've had several photoshoots done here at the Sydney docks." And then Maureen started to cry. "I did this, didn't I?" she blubbered.

With a sinking feeling, Tabi sank back against the headboard and whispered, "God, I hope not."

"How would they know that you were even here though?" Maureen asked, trying to stop the tears.

"The boat, it's registered at the marina."

"And they would have found out the name of the boat, how?"

"I'm sure it hit the news," she said. "The fact that my sailboat went under, and I lost it."

"And I told him about that too," she said. "God, I'm so sorry."

"It's not your fault," she said. "You're one of the most honest, open, bubbly personalities that I know. It's just natural for you to talk about your friends." The trouble was, it really was the way Maureen was built. She didn't have a care in the world about what she said, but it was always good stuff. She wasn't a gossiper, and she wasn't one to backstab. But she absolutely loved to talk, so you could never give her a secret to keep because it was beyond her control. At the same time, this brought up a whole different avenue of investigation.

"I'm really thankful that you called me," she said.

"Honestly I wouldn't be as nice about it," Maureen pouted. "I thought about it all day, and then, as the evening settled in, I just felt worse and worse, and I knew I wouldn't sleep tonight without a full confession."

Tabi chuckled. "It's fine," she said. "The insurance will cover the bulk of it, and I'm in a hotel right now. So it is what it is."

"Well, I hope they cover all of it," she said. "You could use some new furniture."

"So could you," she said, chuckling. "What I really need is to have all this settled."

"And I'm just part of it all now too," Maureen said sadly. "But at least I can sleep now."

"I'm glad to hear that," she said. After she hung up the phone, she stared down at the piece of pie and picked it up and scarfed it down in four bites. It was absolutely delicious. Stunningly good. And she was also now fairly ticked off and upset.

To think that somebody had gone to the marina, where her boat had been, and had found her friend Maureen and had talked to her, chatted her up, even slept with her. He made her feel like she was someone special. Then ditched her after making breakfast plans because he had gotten what he wanted from her. It just made Tabi superangry. Talk about feeling used. She pondered the events and finished off another treat, the TV show blaring mindlessly in the background. She realized that she needed to share this news with Ryland.

She picked up the phone, remembering Cain's comment about not contacting them too early. Frowning, she brought up a text message and typed, **Is this too early?** She quickly typed in what Maureen had said. Her thumb hovered over the Send button for a long time. Then finally she decided they would probably have their ringers off anyway, and he'd see it when he turned it back on again, so she quickly hit Send. Then she settled back, tense and waiting, wondering just what else this asshole might have done to find her. And if he'd found her in Sydney, how much effort would he go through to find her now in Perth?

WHEN RYLAND'S PHONE vibrated, he ignored it, as he studied the alleyway. Their quarry had headed out this direction, within ten minutes of them finding him. Now blended against the back wall, Ryland knew that this guy had somewhat of the same background because he blended in almost as well. But, while Ryland was there, holding his position, Cain had gone around the building and came up on the far side. It was a matter of whether Cain got there before this guy left, or they met up, or if Ryland and Cain could manage to pin this guy in between them.

Ryland hadn't seen any sign of a weapon, but that didn't mean the guy didn't have one. It was almost a given that he would. Nobody out here in this position would be without. Ryland and Cain weren't. Ryland carried a small Glock in his back holster and an ankle piece as well. He hadn't let Tabi see them. This wasn't her world, and he was trying to keep the dark ugliness away from her as much as he could.

That her apartment had been trashed was already a horrific step in the wrong direction. He'd wondered if there would be any retaliation against her, but he couldn't come up with any decent reason why, but Cain was concerned. He felt that, as soon as anybody knew Ryland was alive and talking, they'd be worried about what he would say. Which also meant that Ryland likely saw or noticed something that was important. And, for the life of him, he didn't have a clue what that was or how to figure it out. He heard a faint bird call in the distance and smiled because that meant Cain was in position. Ryland slid down the wall six feet and stopped.

He saw his quarry on the other side of the Dumpster. The suspect blended into the shadows, but his head made just enough of a movement, as he checked from left to right, that it shifted the outline. As soon as it shifted in the opposite direction, Ryland moved forward another six feet. As soon as the target looked back Ryland's way, Ryland stopped, almost feeling the fear rolling off the man. And that was good because the guy should be afraid. He should be damn well good and afraid because this attack on Bullard and the team was just pissing off Ryland.

As soon as the man's head moved again, Ryland moved down another six feet. That was two large steps. When the guy's head shifted one more time, Ryland knew the man was aware he was being hunted. This time Ryland didn't move at all, and he just waited. Out of the corner of his eye, he caught sight as Cain shifted inward.

Finally their target froze and called out, fear lacing his voice, "What do you want?" The fear was interesting because a pro wouldn't have been afraid. A pro would have been angry and stealthy, just looking for a way out.

"You haven't been paid enough for this," Ryland said, his tone conversational.

"Haven't been paid at all," he snapped. "What the hell do you want?"

"Who said I wanted anything?"

"Why are you stalking me?"

"Because it's fun," he said.

"For you, not for me. So get the hell away from me." That raw fear really got to him.

"Why did you go beat the crap out of my girlfriend's apartment?"

"Is that what you call it, like it's a living thing?"

Enough sneering was evident in his voice to suggest that some of his fear had tamped down. "You didn't have to destroy everything," he said. "What did she ever do to you?"

"How do you know it was me?"

"Video cameras."

"No way," he said. "No bloody way."

"Absolutely," he said. "You used a hat and kept your head down, but your profile is pretty hard to miss."

"Damn you," he said.

"No, more like damn you," Ryland said.

The target's head shifted again, and Ryland moved. This time he managed to get to Ryland's side of the Dumpster but he couldn't see where Cain was.

"What do you want?" the man cried out. "I don't have any money."

"Well, of course not. You didn't get paid yet."

"Jesus, how did you get over here?" he cried out nervously.

And, just like that, Ryland was there, gun out, pointing at him. "Hands up," he said.

The guy stared at him, but he was flattened against the wall with a gun in his hand. It was almost as if he were wondering if he could take Ryland on.

"Don't try it," he said. "First, I thought you were a pro, but you're not."

"Pro what?"

"Mercenary," Cain said, suddenly appearing at their side from the darkness.

The guy looked at Cain in shock. "I thought somebody

else was here," he said. "Jesus, you're quiet."

"Oh, there's a lot of us," he said. "When you take on one of us, you take on all of us. So we're trying to figure out if you had anything to do with blowing up the plane." The look on the guy's face was almost comical.

"Plane? I don't know what you're talking about," he said.

"Then you better talk about what you do know," Cain said. "My buddy here, he wants to beat the crap out of you, for what you did to his girlfriend. The fact that you hounded his girl."

"I don't know what you're talking about."

"Now you're just lying," Ryland said, bored. "Let's take him back to the little room we set up for this."

"I'm not going anywhere."

"Says you, but you don't have any say in the matter. We'll knock you out and take you anyway."

"You can't do that," he said.

"You'll stop us?" Cain asked with interest. "That should be fun to see."

"Maybe I will," he said.

"Nice," Ryland said, his silky voice trailing as he eyed the stranger. He shifted ever-so-slightly, so he could confirm the profile. But, once that was in his head, he nodded and said, "I know that you're the asshole who trashed her apartment. So, what I want to know is, who paid you and why?"

"Doesn't matter why," he said. "And honestly I didn't ask."

"And how much did he pay you?"

"Not enough."

"Of course not because now you'll take the fall for it.

How did he contact you?"

"He showed up at my apartment one day," he said.

"And do you have a description?"

"Tall, dark, and handsome."

"Right, so if we're just getting smartass answers out of you," he said, "we might as well leave you broken and bleeding in the alley. That will help us work out some of our frustrations at least."

"What good will that do?" he said bitterly. "I did the job, and I didn't get paid."

"How were you supposed to get paid?"

"Afterward an envelope was supposed to be in my apartment."

"No envelope?"

"Nope."

"You didn't get a hefty deposit first?"

He just shrugged and shook his head.

"Right, so you weren't worth getting paid?"

"I did the job he asked," the guy said. "I should have gotten paid."

"What was the amount?"

"One thousand bucks."

"To mess up an apartment in two and a half hours? That's pretty good wages," Ryland said.

"Maybe he decided you didn't do a good enough job. Was there anything else you were supposed to do?" Cain suggested.

"No, just get in and get out. That's what he said."

"What about the cameras?"

"Well, I don't know how to disable cameras, so I did the best I could. I wore a hat. What else am I supposed to do?"

"And did he ask you to write the message?"

"No, that was me," he said. "I just, you know, really got into it."

"So maybe he got pissed off about that."

"I don't know. He was also looking for something."

"What?"

"Evidence of some boyfriend but I don't know who." He looked at Ryland and said, "You?"

"Maybe," Ryland said cheerfully. "But I didn't get back into town that fast."

"All I did was mess up her apartment, and she's probably got insurance, so what do you guys care?"

"You might be surprised," he said. "Terrorizing innocent young women isn't exactly on our list of how to make friends."

"Well, getting paid is on my list of how to get fed," he said.

"Not really," he said. "All it means is that they didn't want to waste the time and money by giving it to you, so they were planning on taking you out in the meantime."

"Why would they take me out?" he said, his voice rising. "I didn't do anything."

"I don't know about that," he said. "The thing is, you did what they asked, and you saw him. And the minute you saw him—well, that's just a problem."

"But I didn't really see him," he said.

"Why not?"

"Because I was at my apartment, and, when I went to open the door, he grabbed the door on the other side and told me that I wasn't allowed to step out, but that he had a job for me."

"So you didn't actually see him?"

"Not much," he said. "I had my face against the corner,

to try and see him, but his face was right there too, so all I really saw was his eye."

"Interesting tactic," he murmured, and actually it was, because, as long as he could make sure the guy didn't look afterward, it was hard to see anybody when they were eyeball to eyeball. "Accent?"

"Sure, but don't ask me what kind."

"And you were supposed to get an envelope of money afterward? Is that correct?"

"Yes," he said. "But what good did that do because I didn't get it."

"Or your place is such a pigsty that you couldn't find it."

He shook his head. "No, I searched."

"No way to contact him?"

"No," he confirmed.

"Okay then," Ryland said. He stepped back and asked, "Do you have any ties to Africa?"

"Africa? Hell no," he said. "Why would I give a shit about anybody over there. My world is such a mess here now."

"You could try for a job," Cain said mildly. "You know? A real one, where you get up and go to work every day. Just saying."

"Screw that shit," he said. "That's what idiots do. I take on special jobs."

"Special jobs, huh. Well, how did this last one go for you?"

"He's probably just delayed in paying me," he said.

"Maybe and, then again, maybe not."

Cain looked at Ryland and motioned toward the shadows. Ryland said, "Close your eyes for a few minutes."

"Hell no," he retorted.

Ryland reached out and, with a light tap, knocked him out cold.

"Well, I guess he shut his eyes anyway," Cain said.

They left him there, turned, and walked down the alleyway.

"Do you think he knew anything?" Cain asked.

"Nope, he didn't know shit. He's just another stupid little idiot, looking for an easy score," Ryland said.

"On the other hand," he said, "we need more answers."

"We do."

As they got to the end of the alleyway, they stopped at the corner and looked back down to where they had left him. As they turned and headed out toward the traffic, a hard, loud shot came behind them. They looked at each other, and both split, one going left, one going right. Ryland raced around the corner and headed back toward the hotel but in an erratic pattern. The last thing he wanted to do was lead whoever the hell had just killed their stooge back to the hotel. Because going back led them to Tabi, and that wouldn't happen. The fact that somebody had actually followed them, found them behind the bar, and waited until they talked to their guy was already unnerving. So far, they were behind the game, and this asshole was coming out ahead every damn time.

Knowing Cain was somewhere behind him, Ryland quickly ducked into a back door of a Chinese restaurant and made his way to the front, ignoring all the comments from the kitchen staff. Once through there, he bolted out the front of the restaurant and headed down the road where he crossed and disappeared into the shadows of another alleyway. It took him a good ten minutes to work his way back around to the hotel. He stayed in the shadows around the corner, waiting and searching to see if anybody followed him. When he saw nothing, he moved smoothly inside and raced back up to the third floor, the floor that they were on.

As he walked up to the door, Cain approached from the far end. They looked at each other. Cain shook his head and said, "All clear."

Ryland knocked on the door and said, "Tabi, it's us."

They quickly unlocked the door and stepped in.

CHAPTER 10

W HEN THE DOOR opened suddenly, Tabi bolted awake and stared in shock as both men raced in. Her hand to her chest, she gasped out, "Jesus, you scared me."

Ryland came to her side and gave her a quick hug. "It's all good," he said.

She shook her head. "Not if you came running in like you did."

"We had an unexpected visitor," he said, as he sat down on the side of the bed, moving the cart out of the way. He looked at the tray appreciatively. "I see you made good use of your time."

"I also sent you a message. Did you look at it?"

He pulled out his phone. "I did feel it vibrate, but we were a little busy," he said with a smile. He quickly read the message and frowned. "What the hell?"

"Yes, it means that, whoever is after you, actually went to where my boat was moored after finding out about it, presumably from the news, what with your plane going down and my boat sinking," she snapped. "Then he tracked down my girlfriend in Sydney, making her think she was having a hot date, then left her high and dry after getting the information he wanted."

"So then he flew to Perth and hired the guy we were talking to tonight," he said. "He was hired to mess up your apartment but not to leave the message. That was his own improvisation."

"Somebody actually paid him to break in and ruin my stuff?" she asked in outrage. "How the hell does that even make sense?"

"I think it was just a warning. But he did say something about looking for me."

"Great," she said. "That sounds absolutely lovely." She raised her hands in frustration, hopped out from under the blanket, and walked to the window.

Cain said, "We're pretty sure he didn't follow us back."

She looked at him. "*Pretty sure?* Please tell me that you're completely sure."

"Okay," he said. "We're completely sure."

"This is just ridiculous." She walked back to the bed and sagged down. "What now?"

"We need to find out who was behind blowing up the airplane."

"Well, I thought you were looking for old enemies."

"Yes, and that's also why it's important that we talk to your friend. Does she happen to have a photo of him?"

She looked at him in surprise. "Oh, my God," she said, as she picked up her phone and called Maureen. When her friend answered, sleepy and groggy on the other end, she asked, "Maureen, do you have a photo of the guy who you told me about?"

"A photo?" She thought about it and said, "You know, I might. I took a couple pictures because I planned to send them to you, when I told you all about my hot date."

"Well, get off the phone and check," she said. "If you have it, just send it." As soon as she got off the phone, she waited anxiously, and, when her phone buzzed, she looked down and smiled triumphantly. "Look!" she exclaimed, as she held up her phone.

Ryland looked at it and said, "Well, I don't know him." He had a mustache and a bit of a five-o'clock shadow, swarthy skin, and dark black hair. He looked at it again, turned to Cain, and asked, "Do you recognize him?"

Cain walked over, shook his head, and said, "It's a disguise."

"What do you mean, a disguise?" Tabi said, studying the man. "I guess the mustache could be put on."

"And the five-o'clock shadow really throws things off too," Cain explained. "He's wearing sunglasses, and I highly doubt that's his hair color, if it's even his own hair."

She frowned. "But surely the cheekbones, the nose, and chin are good markers?"

"We'll see," he said. "We have somebody we can send this to." Cain nodded at Ryland.

"Would you forward the photo to me, please?" Ryland asked. When she did so, he quickly sent the message to Ice and explained what he needed.

When the phone rang moments later, it was Ice. "I'll get back to you, but it will probably take about four hours. It depends on how long it takes to go through the databases."

"Send me what you can, when you can," Ryland said.

"Have you had any update on Garret?" Ice asked.

"Yes," and he explained what they were doing to keep the brain swelling down.

"That's good news," she said. "Any ideas or any help from the Houston videos?"

"I feel like something was there, in the back of my memory," he said. "Honestly I just can't pull it out. But I feel like somebody was there, talking to Bullard, after we got onto the plane, as he was getting on."

"Maybe," she said, "but we found no feeds on that side of the plane."

"But do we have a feed of anybody around there?"

"Not likely. If that's the case," she said, "we can go interview them at the airport and see if they can put anyone else around the plane."

"That's a good idea," he said. "I'm sending it to you." He quickly forwarded the feed.

She checked it and sent him confirmation that she had it.

He looked at Cain. "They'll check and see if they can find who was working on the plane, then go talk to them."

"Good idea, but I'm pretty sure it'll be a no."

"But maybe this local guy's photo and ID? Maybe it's enough to get more on him."

"Maybe," he said, "but I highly doubt it. Remember that part about being a pro?"

"Yeah, but they didn't hire a pro with him."

"Nope, but he didn't have anything helpful either, did he?"

Ryland reached across, picked up her hand, and said, "Look. I know it sounds like we don't have leads, but we will. We'll keep digging. And I promise I won't let anything happen to you."

"I don't think that's in your control," she said quietly. She looked at the two men and said, "I need to go to sleep now. Are you okay if I stay here on this side?"

"Of course," Ryland said, and his tone turned just as formal as hers.

She pushed the trolley out of the way and curled up a little tighter.

"Don't you want to get under the covers?"

She shook her head. "No," she said softly. "I don't."

And she resolutely rolled over, turned her back to them, and closed her eyes.

RYLAND SLOWLY STRAIGHTENED, moved the trolley outside to the hallway, and, when he returned, he exchanged a glance with Cain.

"You can shower first, if you want," Cain said.

"You go ahead," Ryland said absentmindedly. "I'll take first watch, and I'll get a shower when you're done."

"Good enough." Within ten minutes, Cain was back out and getting ready for bed.

Ryland headed in, knowing that his buddy would be awake for at least long enough for him to have a shower. As he stepped under the hot water, he felt the sting of hundreds of small injuries, adding up together into a mother lode of pain. But he stilled his agony and waited until the heat of the water helped ease his aching body.

When he came out, he would take more painkillers, but, right now, this hot shower was what he needed. By the time he was done and dressed, he felt better but also worse, knowing the painkillers would need twenty minutes to kick in. He stepped out and walked to the small table, wishing out loud that he had kept some of the coffee.

"Order some coffee, if you want," Cain said from the bed.

"I was thinking I would," he said.

"I'm hungry again too."

"You know what the answer is then," he said, as he quickly pulled out his phone and sent the request.

When it came ten minutes later, he walked to the door and said to Cain, "I'm just having coffee."

"Good enough," he answered, and his voice sounded sleepy.

Ryland opened the door, grabbed the trolley, smiled at the waiter, and pulled it inside. As he went to close the door, he froze as he heard the unmistakable sound of a safety flipped off as the silencer on the gun appeared around the door. But he was already reacting, although his reaction time was a little on the slow side. If he hadn't dodged behind the door, those first two bullets would have come right at him.

Cain bolted from the bed, and Ryland already had grabbed the gunman by the wrist, slamming the door, his arm against the doorjamb. Ryland kept pounding the door against the gunman's hand, until he heard bones crack. The gun dropped, and he pulled the waiter in, dropping him to the floor with a hard kick to the gut, and a fist to the jaw knocked him out. Then Ryland dragged him inside and closed the door firmly.

Cain walked closer and said, "Wow, I guess that didn't go so well."

"No," he said. "When I came out of the shower, I left my gun at the door."

"Well, it looks like we're all good and clear, and she's still asleep," Cain said.

Ryland looked to see Tabi still sound asleep, her chest rising and falling with a slow steady rhythm. "Amazing that she can even sleep at all," he said.

"It is, isn't it? But apparently she can sleep through anything," Cain said, with a chuckle.

"What will we do with him?"

"Well, we need answers, but she won't take it very kindly."

Ryland smiled. "Yeah, that's the truth."

"Okay, so let's get another room right beside us," Cain suggested.

With that ordered, he waited until he got a phone confirmation. With instructions to leave the key under their door, he waited until he heard the envelope and then retrieved the key. He picked it up and stepped out into the hallway with his gun in his hand and quickly walked to the door adjacent to them. He opened up that room and then opened up the connecting door between the two.

With that done, he locked the main hallway doors on both sides, dragged the unconscious gunman into the second room and closed it, so Tabi wouldn't hear them. He picked up the guy and tossed him on the bed. Grabbing the ice bucket from the counter, he walked into the bathroom and filled it with cold water, then threw it on him.

The man came awake with a roar, and instantly Ryland hit him again.

He went down, sobbing with pain.

"Scream again," he said, "and I'll just knock you out and throw more ice water on you, until you get the message."

The gunman lay on the bed, shuddering. He held his hand against his chest. "You broke my wrist."

"You tried to kill me," Ryland said calmly. "I really don't give a shit what happens to your wrist. I'll break the other one too, if you don't start giving me answers."

"I was offered ten thousand to take you both out," he said.

"Wow, that's cheap," Cain said. "That's kind of insulting really. It should have been at least ten thousand for each of us."

"Ten thousand extra if I took her out too."

"Wow, we're only five thousand, and she's ten?" Cain said. The two men looked at each other in mock outrage. "That's bullshit. That's what that is," he said. "We should have been that much too."

"For you, it's a joke," the man said. "For me, I need the money."

"A lot of people need the money," Ryland said. "That doesn't mean they turn in their jobs and lose the lifestyle they had. One that had to have been a whole lot easier than a lot of others."

"Sure, the job's okay, but all I see is you guys coming and going, and people like you always have money," he said. "I want to be a little more like that."

"Oh, so you just decided you'll be a gunman?"

"Well, you've got to be doing something right," he said, "because you got money. This place is not cheap."

"It isn't," he said, "but we're also part of a very large team that handles national security all over the world. Why the hell should we be knocked down because some little pissant like you wants to step up in the world without doing the work?"

The guy just looked at him. "You're not criminals?"

"No," Ryland bit off. "We're not."

"He said that you were, that you were stealing from banks."

"Well, we're not," he said, though he tucked away that information. "I don't even know why the hell you would listen to some bullshit like that."

"Because I believed it," he said. "I wanted to believe it though," he added sadly.

"How did he pay you?"

"Cash, ten thousand up-front in my apartment."

"Did you see him?"

"I thought I saw him coming into the hotel one day, when I was just trying to leave. I was going out the front door. I think he was trying to come in."

"Did you hold it open for him?"

At that, the gunman stared. "Well, yeah," he said.

"You do know that nobody is allowed to enter this building without the security required to get in, right?" Ryland asked, shaking his head.

"And I assumed he had it."

"Well, you assumed wrong," Ryland snapped.

"Or," Cain said, "he uses this hotel too."

"Wouldn't that be fun," Ryland said.

"So do you think he just followed you home one day?" Cain asked.

"I don't know. I've never dealt with him before, business or personal. So I assume so."

"Makes sense. He finds out you work here, follows you home, offers you extra money, which is obviously a big incentive because he did his research on you ahead of time. So now what happens to you, now that you failed the mission?"

"I don't know. I don't get the other half?"

"Oh, I suspect it's a lot worse than that," Ryland said. "Let me go back a bit to the last guy he hired, to trash the woman's apartment. They shot him."

"What do you mean, they shot him?" he asked, bolting upright and wincing with pain. He lifted his broken hand, then cried out again and said, "I can't even work now."

"I'm not sure that'll be a big issue for you," Cain said, "because you'll be dead soon too." He looked at Ryland and said, "I'll stay here with him. You go in and look after her."

Ryland nodded. "What do you want to do with him?"

"I say we let him go," he said. "Once we've got all the information we need, that is. They might not kill him today or tomorrow. Likely in the next month though. Can't afford not to get the intel now."

"I don't have any other information to give you," he said.

"Was it your idea to come to the apartment when we ordered something?"

"Well, it made sense. It's not like I'd get past these steel doors any other way," he said.

"Right, that makes sense, doesn't it? So he already knew that we were here."

"He may have gone looking for me, but he already knew all about you."

"That's very interesting too," he said.

"Can I go now?"

He looked at Cain and shrugged. "I say we let him go."

"Sure, let him go. We'll see what he comes up with next."

At that, they stepped back and opened up the hallway door.

"Go, before I change my mind," Ryland said.

The gunman got up off the bed and bolted. And they let him. And half of him wished him well. The other half hoped he died immediately.

Ryland looked at Cain and asked, "Did you get a photo of him, by any chance?"

"Several," Cain said. "You know? This big boss man guy's been ahead of us, every step of the way."

"I know," Ryland said in frustration. "Every damn step."

He turned back to the other room and said, "And we just paid for a second room, for nothing."

"Not for nothing," Cain said. "I'll sleep in here." And he threw himself down on the bed and said, "Go in there, and look after your ladylove."

"Hardly my ladylove," Ryland said.

"Oh, I see sparks," Cain said. "Just keep the lovey-dovey stuff to a minimum, will you?" Pulling the blankets up over him, he rolled away, saying, "You're on first watch, so get at it."

Ryland walked back to the other room, leaving the adjoining door slightly open. At least he had some coffee and treats. He walked in and saw Tabi still asleep. Pushing the trolley against the table, he sat down and brought everybody up to date. He had the phone image that Cain had sent him of their recent attacker, so he sent that to the rest of the team and then on to Ice.

Eton phoned immediately. "You were attacked in that hotel?" His voice was hard and incredulous.

"Not only attacked but the pro knew we were here, and he'd picked up one of the staff."

"I'll have something to say to the management about that."

"Well, the gunman did suggest that the guy who hired him may use the place too."

"Shit," he said. "Is no place safe anymore?"

"Nope," he said. "No place is safe."

"So now they're just trying to kill you outright?"

"Seems like it. Apparently it's important to someone that I drop dead."

"Cain okay?"

"We're both okay," he said. "Unfortunately having to

deal with all that isn't helping our investigation very much, and we're not getting anywhere."

"Maybe not, but hopefully we'll get to the end of this pretty damn fast."

"Did you guys come up with anything?"

"Still no sign of the father. He's gone to ground. We're paying for rumors, and, so far, it's like he's on an agenda. So he's staying on our hot list but no sign of where he is."

"He has a pretty big network behind him too, doesn't he?"

"Very," he said.

"Okay, keep at it. I'm on watch. I'll grab some coffee and see what else I can come up with. We got an angle to research. Ice is doing facial recognition on the gunman visiting Tabi's girlfriend. She already sent me passenger lists. So I want to check flights in and out from Sydney to Perth and see if we can find something." He hesitated, then added, "Ice also said she contacted Bullard's half brother to let him know. He's pretty upset. Said he told Bullard to get out of the business while he still could."

"Good," Eton said. "But him warning Bullard would have been water off a duck's back. Bullard lived and breathed his company."

"You'll know if we come up with anything."

And, with that, Eton hung up.

Ryland quickly searched through the passenger flight lists to Perth, looking for anybody who had come through in the last two days. There were 242 of them. He narrowed that down to single males under forty. That dropped the relevant passengers down to forty-two. Feeling a whole lot more positive on that, Ryland started a search, going through social media and another through the DMV sites for driver's licenses, looking at photos.

Sure enough, he came up with something that looked suspicious—if you took away the mustache and the five-o'clock shadow and made the hair blond. Quickly he took a snapshot and copied the file, then sent it to Ice with a message, asking her to check it out, saying the subject in the photo had flown into Perth that morning.

While she was doing her thing, he got up and poured himself another cup of coffee and snagged one of the very large cookies from the tray. They had used this hotel a lot when they needed it. But it was quiet, unknown, and served to look after a different sector of the population. They needed places like this, but they weren't the only ones. That meant that other people had uses for it too. *God help us.*

Just as he got halfway through the cup of coffee, Ice phoned him. "That's him," she said.

"Perfect," he said.

"He's traveling under a passport in the name of John Green."

He snorted. "Jeez, that's as bad as John Smith."

"No, that's actually better," she said, "but not by much. And I think I have him on a different database."

"Which one?" he asked.

"Interpol."

His back stiffened at that. "Who is he?"

"Hang on," she said, her voice excited.

"It'd be nice to actually get some progress here," Ryland said.

"He's known out of England," she said, "as John Man-chester."

"That sounds like another alias."

"Believe it or not, that's the name he was born under,

but he's gone by John Green, John Smith, John Brown."

"Quite the imagination," he said sarcastically.

"No."

"What do you have on John Manchester?"

"Suspected of the attempted assassination of a cabinet minister," she said. "Twelve years ago."

"Shit, they haven't found him since then?"

"He hasn't surfaced since then and is suspected of working over in Africa. Bingo."

"Well, that puts him in the right location to have something come up with Bullard, but the question is this—was he hired by someone else or is he doing this on his own?"

"That'll be your job to find out," she said. "I suspect when you do find him, it'll be just one piece of a larger puzzle."

"Shit," he said. "That's not what I want to hear."

"No," she said, "but it does make sense."

"If you say so." He hung up quickly and tagged his team with the update.

Eton phoned him. "What the hell is going on here?" he asked.

"I suspect," Ryland said, "that somebody has hired him on. He's a pro and known for doing a lot of high-profile cases." He was reading from the files that Ice had sent him. "Looks like a pretty interesting guy actually."

"Meaning?"

"In another situation," he said, "we would probably hire him ourselves."

"That's not making me feel any better," Eton snapped.

"Nope, but just think about it. Right now, it's all good."

"So, says you."

"Yep, so says me." He hung up.

Just then, he heard, "Ryland?"

He got up and walked over slowly, grimacing. The pain pills had kicked in, but he was stiff and sore from sitting at the table for too long. His body desperately needed a week or two of rest, but no way that would happen right now, so he needed to just shut it out for the meantime. With Cain now awake, it was his turn to rest. He sat down on the edge of the bed, picked up her hand, and said, "Sorry, did I wake you?"

She yawned, looked around, and asked, "What time is it?"

He checked his cell phone. "It's about two in the morning. It's almost time for me to get some sleep."

"You've been up all this time?" she asked, as her eyes widened. "You need to get some rest."

"I'll get it," he promised.

She snorted. "Like hell. You seem to think you're invincible."

"Not really, I do know I need to get rest," he said. "It's just that some things have to happen in their own time."

"Bullshit." She laughed, then turned over and said, "Get some sleep." He gave her a quick kiss on the forehead. "Why do you keep kissing me anyway?" she muttered.

"Because I like it," he said cheerfully. Then he got up, walked to the other bed on the far side of the room, and said, "I'll sleep over here."

She pounded the bed beside her. "Sleep here instead. I'll feel better."

"Are you sure?"

She smiled, nodded, and said, "Absolutely."

He stretched out on the bed beside her, and he pulled the blanket up over him. "Go to sleep then," he said.

"You first," she said, but her voice was sleepy, drowsy

sleepy.

And he just smiled, reached over, hooked an arm around her ribs, and said, "Now sleep."

She gave a big yawn, curled up against his chest, and said, "Okay."

He listened to her deep breathing as it slowed into a steady rhythm. With his arm wrapped around her and his head tucked up on top of hers, there was an idyllic quality to being here together. He closed his eyes and let his mind start to drift. In the other room he heard Cain getting up.

When he walked into their room, he asked, "Is there still hot coffee?"

"Only if it's in a thermos," he joked. "Check that heated thermal pot," he said, "but it's old. So you might want to order new."

"Sleep," Cain said. "I'm a big boy."

"I left you notes over there," he said. "Quite a bit of an update. I ID'd the guy through the flight records. Ice sent over the files, so you'll want to give it a read."

"We got him now," Cain said with excitement.

"Well, at least we know who he is. Catching him? Now that will be tomorrow's trick. I need to get some sleep before that happens."

"Go ahead and sleep," he said. "I'll read through this, and we'll catch up in the morning."

"Will do," Ryland answered, then closed his eyes and sank into the depths of sleep.

CHAPTER 11

TABI WOKE UP, feeling the heat all around her, like she hadn't experienced in a long time. She yawned and stretched, surprised when her arms and legs came up against a warm body. She opened her eyes to find Ryland curled up against her. In fact, she was curled up, and he was curled up all around her. Under the same blanket with her. She lay here, quiet for a long moment, trying to remember what happened.

She did remember speaking to him and telling him to come to bed, and apparently he'd followed orders. She snuggled back and smiled. Careful of his injured arms, he tucked her up closer. As she opened her eyes, she saw that Cain worked in the corner by the window on a laptop. Obviously they'd switched shifts somewhere in the night. She was good with that because, damn it, Ryland was injured, and he shouldn't be working at all. But he was stubborn, and it was clear he wouldn't listen to her. It would take something a whole lot more serious to knock him down. And, if he weren't careful, that would happen.

She waited for a long moment, but finally her bladder demanded that she get up. She didn't want to, but she had no alternative. She shifted from under Ryland's arms, gently patting his hand when he tried to pull her closer. "I have to go to the bathroom," she whispered. He murmured something unintelligible and released his arm.

She slid out from underneath him, smiled at Cain, and walked to the bathroom. There she looked at the shower longingly, used the facilities, washed her face, and stepped out. As she walked back to the bed, Ryland had sprawled out, taking up her space completely. She headed to the table where Cain was. "You're on watch, huh?"

"Absolutely," he said. "Ryland needs more sleep than he'll willingly take, so I'm trying to give him extra."

"What time is it?"

"It's eight or so already," he said with a smile.

"Good," she said. "Maybe he'll sleep a while longer."

"What about you?"

"I was thinking about a shower."

He nodded with approval. "Go ahead," he said. "Take your time, and, when you're out, we'll order up coffee and some breakfast."

"Coffee sounds great," she said, as she tiptoed past Ryland, grabbed her small bag, and headed for the bathroom. There, overjoyed at the opportunity, she stripped down and stepped in for a long, luxuriously hot shower. She shampooed her hair twice and scrubbed down the rest of her. Just something about seeing her apartment torn up gave her a horrible, dirty, and violated feeling, almost something that crept through her skin into her soul.

Finally scrubbed clean, she stepped out with one towel wrapped around her body and another twisted around her hair. She pulled out some clothing, looking to see just what she had available. Dried off and fully dressed, she pulled on socks and her slip-on canvas shoes, then stepped out into the main room. She hung up one wet towel on the back of the door, but left the towel on her head. She walked to Cain, while towel-drying her hair. "Ryland's still sleeping, I see."

"Good," Cain said. "I just put the order in for breakfast."

"And we'll eat it without him?"

Cain gave a light bark of laughter. "Well, we could try," he said. "Although I don't suspect that will work very well."

"Nope, I don't suspect it will at all."

She walked back and hung up the second towel and then joined him again. "So was it an easy night?"

He looked up at her and chuckled at her joke. Then smiled and said, "You have no idea, do you?"

She frowned and asked, "What happened? Where are we?"

"Well, last night we ordered coffee for Ryland, and, when it came, it was delivered by a gunman."

She stared at him, her jaw dropping. "Are you telling me that I slept through a gunfight?"

"Well, he had a gun. We didn't," he said, with a laugh. "Ryland took out the gunman and broke his wrist against the door."

"Jesus," she said. "When will that man ever catch a break?"

"I think he's gotten lots of good breaks. Like right now—you're sweet on him, aren't you?"

She flushed. "I didn't say that."

"You didn't have to," he said, chuckling. "It's obvious."

She shrugged. "I like him, but I'm not sure there's anything more to it than that."

"Well, there is, but we'll see," he said. "Things like this can twist relationships a little bit."

"Maybe," she said. "More than that, I think it just makes you zero in on what's important. It's not like I have time to worry about makeup or fashion. It's more about keeping safe, keeping my energy up, and getting some rest."

"Danger like this," he said, "just takes a relationship down to the basics."

"Is there anybody else you can bring in to help?" Tabi asked Cain.

"Teams upon teams," Cain said. "I've been contacting them all night."

"I suppose they're all across the world?"

"Yes, but also some are on security teams or independents," he said, "and that's just as important. Bullard was highly respected."

"No," she said. "Not by everyone."

He shot her a shuttered look and then nodded. "One point to you."

"This isn't about points but about deaths," she said. "What we have to keep in mind here is that apparently Bullard being shot down hasn't ended this thing. So who all knew that Garret and Ryland were on the plane that day?"

"Anybody who needed to know," he said.

"From what it sounds like, you guys are all about having the right information, and you're not alone. Particularly if you've reached out to other teams."

"I had to," he said. "It's part of what I do for Bullard. I have a massive network."

"Right," she said. "So you extended your reach in order to contact as many people as possible. But what if you contacted the wrong one?"

"I can only presume I did," Cain said. "I'm pretty sure they already knew that Ryland and Garret survived the crash. Otherwise there would have been no reason to go after you."

"That's something I still don't understand. Why go after

me anyway?" she asked.

"Only on the thin possibility that Ryland might have been talking to you about something important. And it could have happened if he were unconscious, in a coma, or talking in his sleep, things like that."

"It's not like we were in a position to be chatting, and, after getting them on my boat, then having to be rescued myself, I was hardly in any condition to be learning any secrets."

"But see? In our business, condition doesn't matter. A loose thread is a liability, and they apparently feel they can't afford that."

"Is your team really going after them?"

"We already are," he said. "This isn't about playtime anymore," he said, his gaze hard. "This is all about getting to the bottom line."

"Well, now you have the guy who trashed my apartment—plus the coffee-bearing gunman who's soon to be dead, and the one who probably shot them both on your radar. How do you find him now?"

"That's all in progress," he said. "Facial recognition is checking all the city cameras, and that will run him down pretty fast. We also have one guy who's dead in the alley." At her look he shook his head and said, "Don't ask."

"Is facial recognition even legal?" Did she even want to know about the other dead guy? No.

"We don't give a shit if it's legal or not," Ryland said, now awake and stiffly moving around the room. "You'll never be safe if we don't find him."

"If you do find him, then will it be over?" At that, the men exchanged a glance. She nodded slowly. "Not likely, is it?"

"It's possible," Ryland said. "I just don't have any real way to know that yet."

"Well," she said, "the answer may well be in the back of your head. You've already mentioned this father and the two guys who worked for you, who then went back to work for the father again."

"Sure, but we—well, we went in after his daughter. It wasn't our fault she'd already been killed."

"Grief has no boundaries," she said solemnly. "I've seen it time and time again. Even though we at the hospital could do nothing at times when the families brought somebody in, it was too late for us or anyone else to deal with it. Yet we were still blamed and called an incompetent medical staff. The families always had something they would cling to, something the hospital did wrong. They're not necessarily bad people. They're just looking for an outlet for their anger and pain."

"This was a year ago," Ryland said.

"Grief knows no time limits," she said.

"It would take a long time to set up something like this," Cain confirmed. "Not the least of which would be waiting for the right opportunity."

"And going to Texas, was that it?" Tabi asked.

"Very few friends are in Bullard's world. Ice and Levi are the ones who he would bend over backward to help. A few others are around the world that he would do the same for, and I've already put out an alert, asking them to stay low and to watch their backs," Cain said.

"Do you think he's trying to take out Bullard, Bullard's inner circle, or everybody in Bullard's network?" she asked.

"Targeting everybody in Bullard's network would be out of reach," Ryland said, joining them with a cup of coffee.

"That's hundreds and hundreds of people."

"So just the team then? How many is that?" she asked.

"Depends on any given day," Ryland said. "Thirty?"

"Have you had everybody, like, check in yet?"

He looked at her with an uncomfortable expression and said, "Not quite."

After a few moments of awkward silence, Cain spoke up. "No word from Garret's brother, Gregg," he said. "He works on another Bullard team, based out of Africa, but Gregg isn't usually this quiet. Especially with Garret in a coma, we expected Gregg to make contact."

Tabi looked at Cain. "Garret's brother works with all of you too?"

He nodded, his voice grim. "He was in Africa, holding down the fort."

"And you've not heard from him?" she asked cautiously.

"No, but, once we activate an alert status, we go into black mode."

"But surely there's a way to contact him."

"I've tried," Ryland said. "Cain too. So all I can do is hold off on thinking the worst and believe in the fact that Garret's brother is very, very capable."

"Is he younger or older?"

"Younger."

She winced at that.

He caught it. "What difference does that make?"

"Older siblings always feel responsible for the younger ones, that's all," she murmured.

He glared at her. "Did you hear me when I said he was capable?" he said. "We taught him everything we know."

"I get it," she said, with a pleading look at Ryland.

Ryland just gave her a half smile. "There's always trade-

offs when your family works with you," he said. "The work
we do is dangerous, and we go black for any number of
reasons, and it can be for weeks or even months."

"I get it," she said. "I hope there's nothing in particular
with this case that sets off any alarms."

"All the alarms are ringing loud and clear," Cain told
her. "And believe me. Gregg wasn't alone at the compound
in Africa. Dave's there and even Kai and maybe a couple
others." He looked at Ryland. "Do we know for sure who's
manning the fort?"

"I got the list from Eton yesterday," Ryland replied.

"Good. Any reason to be concerned?"

"No, the usual players."

"Good enough," Cain said. He glanced back at Tabi and
said, "We're doing what we do best."

She nodded slowly. "So now what?"

"We'll find this guy, Green, and we'll pick him up,"
Ryland said, as he laughed.

"Somehow I'm not sure it'll be that easy," she said.

"No, it won't be easy to find him," he said. "We'll have
to find a way to bring him to us."

"Haven't you already found a way?" she asked. "I'm
right here."

"No way," he said, frowning at her. "We're not using
you as bait."

"You should," she said. "I'm already a target. What's the
difference?"

Ryland looked to his partner for back up, but Cain nodded, saying, "She's got a point there."

"But he won't be taken in by that," Ryland said. "He'll
know it's a trap."

"No, probably not, so what can you do to sweeten the

pot?" Tabi asked.

"Bring more of the team in," Ryland said thoughtfully.

"Exactly," she said. "Bring in the team, so it looks like they're here to protect me. Then set us up someplace visible and have him give it a go."

"You realize you could die?" Cain asked, his gaze curious and yet interested.

"Well, I will die at some point regardless," she said. "Unfortunately that's the one guarantee that comes with birth, and I have a fairly pragmatic attitude about death, after seeing it on a day-to-day basis."

"Right, I guess your profession doesn't keep you in an insulated tower either, does it?"

"No," she said, "and I have no illusions. Honestly that is one of the reasons I go sailing every year to honor my brother. Because—while you'd like to think that you have years, hopefully eighty or ninety of them—too often, you only get a small fraction of that. Learning to live every day is a huge part of what I attempt to do with my life."

"I like that," Ryland said. "A lot actually."

"Come sailing with me some time," she said, with a smile. "We can go back and revisit where you crashed."

He laughed at that. "I wouldn't mind," he said. "My view of the place is a little distorted."

"Yeah. Like, from my vantage point, you were lying there, with a bunch of garbage hanging around, and your hand on Garret, to make sure he didn't fall."

He looked at her curiously. "Was my hand on him?"

"Well, that's not quite the right phrase," she said. "Your fingers were hooked into his belt. One of the things that got to me was the fact that even though you were about to slip off into the water yourself, you made sure that he was staying high."

"He was hurt," he said.

"So were you, but he was unconscious. That was the difference."

He just gave a shrug and dismissed it.

But she wouldn't let it go so easily. "It just says a lot about who you are."

"It says a lot about my relationship with Garret," he corrected. "We have each other's back."

She gave him a ghost of a smile. "Don't like being a hero, do you?"

At that, Cain burst out laughing. "And that's a little bit of a sore spot with us too," he said. "In a good way."

She looked at him and frowned.

"Bullard is really close to Levi and Ice, and they ran a compound out of Texas. They still do," he said. "They've had a huge matchmaking scenario going on with their team—meaning, a lot of their men have come up with partners, like romantic partners, through their missions. And each time the *hero* comment tends to solidify where the future of the relationship is headed."

"Every woman wants a hero," she said. "The real truth is that heroes can be male and female. The real heroes, those who matter, are the ones who go about life, without requiring accolades, awards, or money. It's the ones who help little old ladies cross the road, who stop in at the hospital to visit somebody without family after surgery, who always have a few extra dollars to quietly help someone out. It's the ones who see a single mom carefully choosing the bare minimum at the grocery store, while the kids can't take their eyes off the meat counter, who slips her a few bucks, so they all can live a little. The heroes are everyday people. I see them all the time, and I've always figured the best thing I could do in life was to be one of them." At that, she fell silent, turned, and said, "Gosh, I don't want to get all maudlin," she said. "It would be really great if we didn't have to sit here in the hotel room all day."

"We aren't," Ryland said. "We've been having pretty heavy discussions once I tossed your idea at the gang."

"Good, and I'm sure they jumped at it."

"They did," he said. "I'm the one fighting it."

"That's because you feel guilty," she said with a knowing smile. "I saved you, so naturally you want to save me. But that's not the way the world works. In a perfect world it would, but this is far from a perfect world."

"I also don't want my whole team to go up in the same blast."

She thought about that. "Explosives. Yeah. It can't be in the open either because they may have snipers. Can't be in a building, as they'll take it down. So what are the options?"

Cain spoke up. "Stealth."

"So enough of the team in and enough of the team out?" she asked.

"Something like that," he said, "and the decoy has to be in a public place, where it's much harder to place bombs, and it needs to be fireproof."

"Does that even exist?"

"The compounds that Levi and Bullard handle," Cain said, "they're all fireproof for just that reason."

She shook her head. "I'm not sure about the world you live in," she said. "However, I'm sucked into it now, and I really hope you can pull this off and get us all out."

"IT'S A SHITTY idea," Ryland said, in a conference call twenty minutes later. He was very aware of the fact that Tabi was lying on the bed, watching movies on her laptop. She also had a headset on, so she didn't have to hear anything that they were talking about. They'd been working on what they needed to do, and she was counting on them doing it. That kind of trust was amazing, but it was also difficult. It was a burden to bear, but no more of a burden than what he'd already accepted because she had saved his life, and he did feel responsible.

"It's a good idea though," Eton said, on the other side of the call. "Like she said, she's already targeted."

"We can't protect her 100 percent," Ryland said.

"Interesting," Eton murmured.

"What do you mean, interesting?" Ryland asked, as he glared at Cain across the table.

A whisper of a smile crossed Cain's face, which quickly disappeared.

"Well, it means that you care," Eton said. "Because, if it were some other woman, you'd have been right up there with us, putting her front and center."

"Well, I would hope not," he said.

"Bullard is missing, presumed dead. Garret is in the ICU and may or may not recover, and you've been badly injured. For all we know," Eton said, "the rest of us are in the line of fire as well."

"Well, you know you probably are," Ryland said, "and I agree with bringing you here. Green will most likely send everybody after us, to try and take us all out."

"So we give him the opportunity," Eton said, his voice turning hard. "Decision made. You've been overruled."

"Who made you boss?" Ryland snapped.

"While Bullard's down, I am," Eton said, his voice cool. "If you've got an argument with that, wait until I get there, and you can try to punch me in the face. But you won't succeed, given all the injuries you've got."

"I'm fine," he snapped.

"I saw the medical report, man," Eton said, his voice softening ever-so-slightly. "Listen. We'll look after her."

"You can't promise that," Ryland said, as he pinched the bridge of his nose, because, of course, there were no guarantees in any of this. A storm was about to happen, but he also knew that it was likely the best chance they had of getting this guy.

"We need him alive," Eton said.

"We'll do our best, but you know that, if our positions were reversed, no way we'd be taken alive." Ryland hung up at that point. Because, of course, it was true. He looked at Cain and said, "I'll go for a walk."

"Stay inside," Cain murmured.

He got up and stormed from the small room. He understood her feeling of needing to do something, anything to get out of the cramped quarters, but it really had nothing to do with the room itself and everything to do with the situation. Choosing the roof, he took the elevator as far as he could and then took the fire escape out onto the rooftop. There was no patio, no walkway, no nothing, just gravel, tar, and lots of HVAC system pipes. And that was fine. It just about suited his mood too.

He wandered carefully, staying close to the pipes, just in case a sharpshooter was out here, not that it would have made a whole lot of sense. But, so far, the bad guys have been one step ahead, and Ryland was done with that. Finally, his temper calmed, he accepted that this really was the best answer to bring the situation to a fast conclusion. He sent Cain a text message and typed **Fine. I'm in.**

Cain responded. **Already in progress.**

Ryland put his phone in his pocket and grumbled, "Of course it is." He sat down against one of the large silver pipes and studied the city around him. Picking up his phone again, he sent a quick text to Cain, asking him to make sure that Garret was under guard.

Will do came the quick response.

Ryland looked around, checking out places to set up for snipers. They needed a public but not too public place for Tabi to be set up as bait. It had to be casual and unaffected. Because Green would just know that it was a setup. But it would also be too big of a pot for the pro to ignore. Was it just the one guy, Green? Would he hire local muscle? Or would Green be part of a bigger team of his own?

It would take a bigger team for Green to take out all of Bullard's team, and they were all in for this one. People were flying in to help from all over the world. Everyone coming owed Bullard their life in one way or another. The fact was, there had been no word on Bullard at all. Ryland thought about that and then sent another message. **And put out an APB, just in case there's any sign of Bullard anywhere.**

Dude, it's already out there. We haven't ever let up looking for Bullard. Stop worrying.

Nope, not happening.

Then worry about your own sorry ass, Cain wrote. **Because, as much as we'll look after her, we can't cover for you too.**

There'll be no covering for me. This time he was so pissed, he dialed Cain and said, "Damn you for saying that, by the way."

"Good, get angry," Cain said. "Get mad, but make sure you come with your A-game on," he said. "Otherwise we'll put you in the same category as her, as one to be protected. And that'll get pretty ugly."

"That won't happen."

"Then get on board with the plan or get the hell off." And, with that, Cain hung up on him.

CHAPTER 12

I T WAS ACCIDENTAL that one of her earbuds fell out as Cain was snarling into the phone. She'd knew, just by what he was saying, that Ryland was on the other end. She kept her gaze locked on her laptop, so Cain wouldn't know that she'd heard anything. And she quickly put the earpiece back in. Better that they didn't know she'd seen a bit of how the dynamics played out. Seemed like Ryland was really pushing, but then he was also quite injured. It would be a terrible blow to his ego to even consider being put in the same category as her.

She lifted her head and gazed across the room. Ryland had already done so much that it would be a shame if they left him out in the end. She looked at Cain to see him staring at her. She removed both earbuds. "Don't leave him out, please," she said softly.

For all the hard-ass he appeared to be, as he looked at her, his gaze was soft. "If he comes up to snuff, we won't," he said. "But we can't have him fighting us at every turn. He can't be a liability."

"I get it," she said. "You're the badass, carrying the worries of the world, but he's got nine fractures. If you don't give him a chance to do this, to pay me back somehow, it'll eat away at his soul."

"I know that," Cain said, as he ran his fingers through

his hair. "I never intended to say it, but he needs a wake-up call. He has to get on board and quit fighting against the plan, or he becomes a liability we can't afford."

"Got it," she said, as she put her earbuds back in, and determinedly flicked through the movie options again, looking for anything to take her mind off what was happening. Then realized she was starving again. "How about a food coma? Coffee and food couldn't hurt, right?"

He looked at her, smiled, and said, "I guess that's an easy answer, isn't it?"

"It's something," she said. "Bring him a meal too."

"Well, I suspect he'll be storming in ready to kick my ass any minute now anyway."

"I don't," she said. "If it were me, I'd be out looking to see how I could contribute. I'd be assessing buildings, locations, looking for where a sniper could be positioned, vehicle access, and all that. I don't really know what your terminology is, but any time I've been talked down to and accused of not pulling my weight, I dove in 300 percent, to make sure such slander could never be expressed in my direction again."

He looked at her with respect. "Glad to hear that," he said. "Looks like the two of you are well matched."

She stared at him, startled. And then nodded. "We are, I guess," she said. "Not sure how we got to this place or where it'll go. I guess it depends on what happens after this little meetup you've got planned."

"The thing is," he said, with half a smile, "we might have a plan, but that doesn't mean that we can count on the other party playing along the way we hope."

"Well, they wouldn't be adversaries of yours if they would play along nicely."

"What do you mean?" he asked, curious, even as he texted. He had found himself intrigued by the different perspectives she brought.

"I mean, if they were adversaries, and they were any weaker or less skilled, you would have taken them out already. The fact that you haven't means that they are up to your skill level, and they will be looking for this."

"Absolutely," he said. "I'm glad that you understand that."

She settled back into the movie, her mind still storming around corners, realizing she needed to acknowledge everything that had happened to her. She opened up a document and started typing, describing everything that had happened to her since she'd gone out for that fateful sailing trip. That's funny because nobody had even asked about the bag that she had taken off the sailboat. And it was still with her. She glanced at it, time and time again, and then finally, when she couldn't put it to rest, she got up, setting aside her laptop. Walking over, she pulled her bag out and searched through it to make sure it was still there. When she pulled out the tiny patch, she smiled and gave it a good rub against her arm. As long as it was still here, she was good.

"And what is that?" Cain asked.

Just then the door burst open, and Ryland came in. "Here I am, with the trolley of food," he announced.

She looked at him, smiled, and said, "That was my request."

He nodded, saw the item in her hand, and asked, "What's that?"

She stared down at it, shrugged, and put it back in her bag. "Something that's important to me, that means nothing to anybody else."

"Which just makes it all the more interesting," Ryland said, walking up behind her. "May I see?"

She hesitated, then nodded, and pulled it back out again.

"It's a Boy Scout badge," he said. And across the top in hand embroidery was the name Lucas. He still didn't look at her, as he asked, "Your brother's?"

"Yes," she said. "He gave it to me when I got the sailboat to keep on board for good luck."

"And you managed to get it off when the boat went down?"

"Remember when everybody was yelling at me? Maybe you don't though," she said. "It was not only chaotic but it was all about getting you off safely."

"I remember you going back under, but I didn't really register how or why." He tapped it gently and stroked his finger across the embroidered name. "Did you do that?"

"Yeah," she said. "Pretty clumsy, isn't it?"

"No," he said. "It's very, very special. I'm really glad you got it off the boat."

Her throat choked up with tears, as she smiled, nodded, and said, "I'll be sure to put it on my next sailboat too." Then she put it back into her bag.

He gave her a gentle squeeze and said, "Absolutely, and I'll take you up on that offer by the way."

She looked at him in surprise.

"To go sailing. Remember?"

She smiled. "Yeah, and I can show you a few of our favorite haunts."

He nodded, and, pointing to the food, he said, "How about we eat now?"

She smiled and caught Cain looking at the two of them and realized he'd heard the conversation. She shrugged, looking at Cain, and said, "Guess you had to be there."

"I'm sorry I wasn't," he said. "I could have made it easier on both of you."

"Or," she said, "you could have been another one for me to look out for."

At that, Cain burst out laughing. "Another point to you," he said.

Feeling happier, she turned her attention to the food. She found great big sandwiches, like Reubens, with sauerkraut and some meat. "I don't know what it is," she said, "but I'm already loving it." And the three of them sat down and ate a wonderful meal, the earlier tension dispelled.

By the time lunch was over, she yawned and said, "I'll have to have a nap, especially after that heavy carb load."

"The bed is all yours," Ryland said. "Or, if you'd rather have a little more privacy, you can use the other room."

"That's Cain's room," she protested.

"No," Cain said. "It's just a room."

"Good point," she said, as she hesitated and then nodded. "Maybe I'll have coffee when I get back up again."

"We'll order a fresh pot when you get up," Cain said.

She smiled, grabbed her bag, and headed into the other room. She went to the bathroom, washed her face, and, taking the bed that Cain hadn't been lying on, pulled back the top blanket and curled up underneath. When she couldn't sleep immediately, she got up, found her bag, and pulled out the little Boy Scout badge. She kept it curled up in her palm, as she laid back down, and this time she nodded off.

"SHE'S GOT A bite to her," Cain said with a smile. "I like

that."

"Only toward you apparently," Ryland said.

"I keep pissing her off," Cain said.

"I can't. I don't want to go there," he said. "She's done too much for me."

"And she's right," he said. "There's a good chance that, if I'd been on that plane, I'd have been another casualty to deal with. You did good with Garret," he added abruptly. "I had no idea you had to hold on to him all that time."

"The jury's out on how good it was," he answered, thinking about Garret, still unconscious. He glanced at his longtime friend and said, "How much of the planning is in place?"

"A lot of it," he admitted. "We're looking for a location."

"I was thinking of the museum," Ryland noted. "It's closed on Sundays, except for private viewings."

"And why would we get a private viewing?" Cain asked.

"Actually a private viewing is already established for a movie star in town," Ryland continued. "I know the security guard who's looking after her. I phoned him, and he said that they'd be quite happy to avoid this private showing. He said he'll show up, make sure that they have access for themselves as scheduled, but, instead of her, we'll suggest that Tabi goes."

"Interesting," Cain said, getting a slightly unfocused look as he contemplated the parameters. "That just might work."

"Of course it wouldn't be great if we shot the place up," Ryland said. "Some glass art display is going on there right now. But the museum has a lot of entrances and exits, and we'd need a lot of people, providing a lot of coverage. With only the two of us here, we'd be short," he said. "But we can easily pull in nine more, if we need to."

"We have sixteen coming already, about two hours out," Cain said.

"Good. Tomorrow's Sunday, so that timing works too."

"Except that somehow we have to let Green know."

"Yeah," Ryland said. "I might have done something about that."

Cain gave him a hard look. "What did you do?"

"I went back to her apartment and left a message on the mirror underneath the first one."

"Interesting," he said. "What did you say?"

"*Catch us if you can*," he said.

"You gave the tiger's tail a shake, huh? I like it," Cain nodded. "And what makes you think he's watching?"

"Because I made sure the cameras all around had a good view of who I was," he said. "You know that shiver down your spine you get when you're being watched?"

Cain nodded.

"It was there," he said. "It's not him watching, but it's somebody. And somebody will have already gone into that place and checked to see what I was doing there."

"Let's find out," he said, and Cain brought up her apartment building cameras, logged into the system illegally, and checked it out. "Look at that," he said.

They watched as the neighbor from across the way opened her door a bit as Ryland walked past. She then shut her door as he went into Tabi's apartment. When he left, she poked her head out and then quickly slipped down to Tabi's apartment.

"She had a key." *At least the landlord did fix the lock.* "So she's in on it," Ryland said. "We'll have to make sure we pick her up."

"Yeah, I'm sending Eton that message."

Just then the camera showed the woman leaving Tabi's apartment, her phone in her hand, and raced back to her apartment.

"I wonder if Tabi knows who she is."

"She probably does," Ryland said. "She's been there for five years. Doesn't mean that she knows anything about it all though."

"No. We never really know about our neighbors anyway," Cain murmured.

"I'll reach out to Ice and see if she can track down who this woman is," Ryland said, as he quickly sent the information. "Do we know what apartment number it is?"

Cain zoomed in on the cameras and said, "It's 341."

"Oh, can you email Ice that snippet of video?" Ryland asked, texting Ice as he spoke.

"Done," Cain said. "Will you tell them?"

"I will," he said, "but after our museum ploy is over. Because you know that Levi and Ice would already be on their way over here."

"Only if there's anything they can do here that they can't do from the compound."

"I don't really want Levi or Ice in the middle of anything anymore," he admitted.

"Because of the baby?"

"Yeah," he said. "She shouldn't be leaving the compound at this time."

"No, not when she has a lot of very good men we could use," he said. "What are they up to now, twenty-five or so?"

"She was talking about two more, so I don't know the accurate tally," he said. "But this is Bullard we are talking about here." He stared at Cain.

Cain nodded, fully understanding.

Ryland broke the stare and, by the time he finished texting, Ice was already calling.

She said, "Stone's on the apartment lady."

"News on Bullard?"

"Nothing."

"Damn."

"I know. Sorry."

"He's a tough old bird. Don't give up. Look at what his half brother, Blachard, went through. And he's fine."

"Well, maybe he's fine. Five years as a prisoner was a hell of an ordeal. Not hard to understand he's out of the business now. He wants nothing to do with it. He worked for Bullard at one time, but now he wants to sit and smell the roses. I can hardly blame him for that." At that, their phones fell silent. "I asked Terkel too."

Ryland stilled. "And?"

"He said, *Bullard's still alive. And to keep looking.*"

"Shit. Well, that's good news and bad. Too bad Terkel can't give us more than that."

"I know. He's also saying what I want to hear, so I don't know if it's safe to trust him." With that, she hung up.

He put his phone down, picked up his coffee, and took a long sip as he stared out the window.

Cain asked, "So this thing with Tabi, it's for real, huh?"

"Is anything ever real?" Ryland answered.

Cain asked again, "It's just so damn fast."

"It's hard not to have special feelings for a woman who saved your life."

"Is that all it is?"

"No," he said quietly. "The more I know, the more I

love."

Cain nodded. "Thought so."

"Also the fact that it's mutual is pretty amazing. I didn't really believe in love at first sight."

"How about love at first saved?" Cain said humorously.

"Maybe," he said. He got up, walked to his bag, pulled out his meds, and took them with a swig of coffee.

"How bad is it, man?"

"It's not great," he said. "These will knock it down though. Don't worry. I'll be there."

"You know I had to say that earlier."

"I know," Ryland said with a nod. "You did. I get it, and I'd have done the same thing if it were you."

"Well, let's hope you don't have to," he said. "I don't have a guardian angel to sit at my bedside and to make sure I come back out of it."

He looked at the door between the two of them and said, "I don't want to think of her not making it through this."

"I told you. That won't happen."

"You'll do your best," Ryland said. "So will I. But there's no guarantee. You know it."

"No," he said. "But, like she said, there's no guarantee for any given day. You guys could go off to your little idyllic town, buy a sailboat, and then get hit by a bus before you ever get on it."

"I know. I think that's one of the reasons we hit it off as well as we did. Just that understanding that we have only today. Tomorrow? *That* we have no guarantees for."

"So let's deal with what we've got to deal with," Cain said. "I brought up the blueprints."

"Now if we only had a printed copy."

"Should be appearing at the door any minute."

At that, there was a noise, just a slight shuffle. Ryland looked to see a large blue piece of paper sliding underneath. "Love this place," he said, as he walked over and picked it up, while Cain cleared off the table. "Except when the guy with the food cart tries to shoot me." They both had a good laugh at that.

Cain laid down the blueprints and smiled. "Look at this," he said. "There are six exits."

"Including the roof, yes." And they started to mark them off.

"Sharpshooters in each one?" Cain asked.

"I'm not sure we want to even leave it to that. You're still out in public," Ryland said. "In which case, a sharpshooter will have to deal with crowds."

"This is a shipping dock," Cain said. "So that's definitely one we have to watch out for." Just then Cain heard his phone buzz. "Eton's hacked into the gallery's security system to check it out."

"Good, we'll be out of time, and we have to make sure the word gets out there."

"It's already out there, but now that Green knows, we have to set it up better than he does. Do we know anybody else who works there?" Cain asked Ryland.

"Maybe," Ryland said.

Knowing that this was Ryland's area of specialty, Cain said, "Reach out to the museum board to see if you know anybody."

Ryland studied the board members, clicking through relationships, then suddenly smiled. "We have a governor," he announced.

Cain looked up and said, "Good people in high places

help."

With that, Ryland placed a call to the governor, and, when George's voice—that highbrow British accent twisted with Australian—came on the line, he said, "It's Ryland."

Immediately the other end became businesslike. "What's up?"

"I'll give you the short version," he said. "Bullard has been potentially taken out of the scene."

"What?" There was a horrified whisper on the other end. Because the governor hadn't been above utilizing Bullard's services in the past. "Are you serious?"

Ryland quickly gave him a synopsis of what was going on. "So now we're expecting tomorrow to be the time frame."

"And why did you have to pick the museum?" he wailed.

"Because the chances of it getting blown up are pretty small. It's pretty well fireproof. It's central and private, yet not private."

"And it also houses incredible works of art."

"Of which a lot are being cleaned and have left the building right now," he said.

The governor stopped and said, "Oh, you're right. That and the computer system is undergoing an upgrade."

"Well, we're already into the security system, so it looks like you need it."

"What, already?"

"Of course," Ryland said, with a laugh.

"What do you need from me?"

"Access," he said, "and now."

"For what?"

"Entrances and exits, places to make sure we've got everything covered, and extra security as far around as we can go."

"How many you expecting?"

"We don't know," he said honestly. "It could be one man. It could be one man with some local men, or it could be a full-on pro team."

"All just to take out you and this woman?"

"No, they'll know by now that Cain's here too," he said, "and, in this instance, they'll also know that we're bringing in the bulk of a team."

"So they'll try and take out as many of Bullard's men as possible."

"It appears that's his goal, and he's already trying to make that happen, so we're drawing him out."

"What an asshole," he said.

"We're setting up security for Garret at the hospital too."

"Garret. God, I hope he pulls through," the governor said. "My son loves that guy."

"I know. We all do," he said, "but, first things first, we need access, so we can get set up."

"You got it. It's shutting down at two o'clock this afternoon, so in about three hours. I'll have them close it a little early, make sure everybody is out. Then I'll get you the keys."

"Don't worry about the keys," Ryland said. "We'll take over the security system and implant a few new cameras for our own use."

"I can't believe you can do that," he groaned. "Did I say we were upgrading it?"

"Yeah, but it won't be enough," he said, "but at least it will make you feel better." With that, Ryland rang off, leaving the governor still spluttering.

Cain looked over with a raised eyebrow.

"We'll have access at two this afternoon. He would give us the keys, but I told him not to bother."

Cain gave a shout of laughter. "Everybody in their ivory towers needs to believe that they have some control."

"And yet, in reality, they have none at all," Ryland replied.

"So true," he said. Hearing a sound, he looked over and there was Tabi, leaning against the doorjamb.

"A governor now?"

"Friends in high places. Remember?"

"And this is all about Ryland's reach?"

"If I have to, I can go to some of the royalty around the world, but, generally speaking, the less they know, the better," he said. "They just want to know people like us are out in the world to keep everything on the straight and narrow."

"What do you do when the government ones are those who go off the rails?"

"That's much tougher," he said, "but it happens. Not every presidential campaign is honest and upright, and a lot of liars, cheaters, and scumbags are out there, filtering through government everywhere. It's more than we can do. Not to mention the fact that we're still only a handful of men."

"Right," she said, with a murmur. She looked down at the pot and asked, "Is the coffee still hot?"

"Doesn't matter," he said. "We'll need more coffee and lots of it."

CHAPTER 13

THE NEXT FOUR hours passed in a blur, and, while Tabi understood a lot of what they were doing, she just didn't understand how. The fact that they had access to the museum from inside and outside just blew her away. "Will we go there today?"

"Yes, once another hour has gone by," Cain said. "To check out the site, set up more cameras, get a feel for the place."

"Am I coming?" Both men hesitated; then she looked at them and said, "Interesting."

"We don't want to leave you alone here," Cain said.

"Ah." She nodded. "Then take me with you, if that makes sense."

"Or not," Ryland said. "It depends on the team."

"Meaning, you need more men here, just to look after me."

"In this case," Ryland said gently, "I'd stay and look after you, but I'm not sending Cain out there alone."

She gave him a brief smile. "Okay, that sounds better." She didn't want Ryland going out there either. But she also knew she'd insult him terribly if she said anything.

When an odd buzz sounded on Ryland's phone, he looked down at it and said, "Hey, they're here."

Cain got up and said, "We'll do twenty-minute check-ins."

She looked at Cain and asked, "Are you coming back?"

"Of course," he said. "In a few hours." And, with that, he walked out.

She walked to Ryland, and, when he opened his arms, she stepped into them. Always mindful of his injuries, she held him close and whispered, "What if they're killed?"

"Like you said, there's absolutely no guarantee of tomorrow. But we'll do our damnedest to make sure that doesn't happen."

She nodded and said, "All of this"—as she pointed to the blueprints covering the table—"how does he remember it all?"

"It's what Cain does. He's a numbers guy and has not quite a photographic memory, but, on things like this, and navigational themes, Cain's gifts are turned on all the time."

"That doesn't sound too bad," she said.

"Well, it's definitely a cross to bear in some ways," he said, "because we all get tired of his insufferable rightness."

She burst out laughing. "Okay, so what are we supposed to do while they're gone?"

"I'm actually running command central," he said. "It's not that I'm doing nothing, but I'll just rearrange some of this."

"Why don't we put it up on the wall?" she said.

He looked at her, surprised, and said, "That's a good idea, but I don't think we have anything to put them up with."

"Are you telling me that you can't get tape?"

"Actually," he said, "I probably have some tacks."

She watched in amazement as he pulled out a small tin and opened it. "Why would you have those?"

"You never know what you might need." With her help, they quickly put up the four blueprints. One for each of the four stories of the museum.

"Good," she said. "Now the table is empty, and you can have it for your work."

"And what will you do?"

"It's been hours since we ate," she said. "I'll put this trolley outside for them to take away, then figure out what I want for dinner. That, obviously, is, well, you know, a fairly major job."

He laughed. "You do that."

She pushed the trolley carefully to the door and asked, "Is it okay to open it?"

He looked over, smiled, and said, "Yes. We have an extra guard or two on the building."

She just shook her head at that, opened up the door, put the trolley outside, and took a good long look down the hallway. Dark burgundy carpet was on the floor, and the wall had an interesting shade of beige, with some pattern on the top one-third of the wall. A very classy look, not ornate or elaborate, just businesslike and subdued. She quite approved. She counted six doors that she saw. She contemplated that.

She slowly closed the door, turned, and looked at him. "Did you ever consider that he could be in one of these rooms?" she asked, as she motioned out into the hallway.

"There is no way to check that," he said.

"What? Can't you just hack into the hotel registration system?"

"No," he said. "It's one of the hotels that we actually worked with to upgrade their security system, so that, so far, it's hack-free."

"That wasn't very smart of you."

He gave a laugh. "Generally they're on our good guys' list."

"But you already had one gunman here. Another instance where they'll owe you."

"Maybe," he said, with a smile.

She asked, "Shouldn't you ask them?"

"I was thinking about checking in a different way," he said.

"And how does that work?"

"Sometimes it works well. Sometimes it doesn't work at all."

"I like it," she said. "So give it a shot." She waited, while he clicked away on the keyboard. "Well?"

"Well, nothing," he said. "The photo that I sent them isn't matching anybody."

"Does that mean that he's here or not here?"

"It means that the photo was never used to identify a current resident. Doesn't mean that's the photo they booked under either though."

"You guys have to give facial ID?"

"Actually the only people who stay here are people they have files on."

"Interesting, but pretty hard to run a business that way."

"Yes, and no," he said. "It's one way."

The evening passed slowly. She ordered in salmon and veggies for dinner, and they had a nice quiet meal, just the two of them, slowly getting to know each other.

"Did you mean it?" he asked.

"Mean what?" she asked, as she laid down her knife and fork and put her plate back on the trolley.

"About going sailing?"

"Absolutely," she said. "Of course I don't have a boat yet."

"Will you get another one? I thought you were wondering about it."

"I think everybody wonders about not getting a new one, when something like this happens," she said. "But it's beyond me to not have another sailboat. Maybe I'll get something different this time."

"I'm sure we could look at it, after this is all over with."

"Yeah," she said. "Just in time for me to go back to work." She winced at that.

"Well, maybe you can take a sabbatical, like a few months off?" She looked at him in surprise. He shrugged. "A couple weeks maybe?"

"I'm not sure," she said. "It's always so busy at work."

"Understood." And he left it at that.

By the time it was bedtime, she was yawning again. "So where should I go to sleep, where I won't disturb you?" she said.

"I would suggest you go back to the bed you took your nap on."

She thought about it and said, "I'd rather be out here, you know, with you."

"Then take that bed," he said.

She nodded and said, "Is it okay to take a shower?"

"Go for it."

As she headed into the bathroom, she called back, "Still no word?"

"Nothing beyond the regular check-ins," he said. "It's all about waiting."

"And you didn't find Green's face anywhere, on any of the cameras in town?"

"Nobody's reported back on it yet, and they'll only report back when the searches are done or if they found him on a camera somewhere."

"Great," she muttered and headed for the shower. It would be a long damn night. The trouble was, she was wrong. By the time she came out after her shower, she walked to the bed and crashed. The last thing she remembered was whispering, "Good night."

"Good night. Tomorrow's a whole new day."

"I hope so," she said. "Let's make it a good one." She closed her eyes and immediately was out like a light.

RYLAND, ON THE other hand, knew that he needed to get some sleep but couldn't afford to be down too long. Just then Cain tagged him and said, "Grab some sleep. We're all set up here, and I'm coming back."

"I'll wait up until you get here."

"Walking down the hallway now."

"Good."

Cain arrived moments later, mentioning food.

"You didn't get to eat?"

"No." And he wasn't alone.

Ryland smiled as Eton walked in. The two men gripped arms in silence, as they noticed that Tabi was sleeping.

"Get some sleep," Eton said. "We'll go to the other room. You've got four hours."

When the two men silently moved to the other room, Ryland settled on the bed beside Tabi, wrapping an arm around her and holding her close. One of the hard lessons in this life was enjoying every moment, and he would enjoy just holding her. The soft scent of whatever shampoo was in the bathroom drifted up. Her hair was wet, and yet she smelled so fresh, so innocent.

That she'd been touched by all this violence was a shame. The work they did was something that 99 percent of the population didn't even know existed. They didn't want to know it existed either. It kept them safe and happy in their quiet little worlds. Before long he felt his fatigue dragging him under, but the pain kept poking at him. Barely shifting, he grabbed his pain pills, took two, and settled down to sleep.

Four hours later, when his shoulder was touched ever-so-lightly, he opened his eyes to see Cain standing there.

"I need four," he said. "Are you up for that?"

Nodding, he got up and walked a bit to stretch, then looked to see Eton crashed on the far bed in the other room. He checked to see if the coffee was still hot, but it wasn't. He wondered about ordering more and then decided to hold off. The more traffic up and down this hallway just said that somebody was awake right now.

Something about the question Tabi had asked earlier poked at him still. What if somebody else in this hotel was involved? And while he'd told her that he didn't have a way to get into their fortified database, the truth of the matter was, they were all pretty high-end hackers. Himself included.

As he sat down to study the database and see what he could find, Ice contacted him. "She's a single mom, two kids."

"Shit," he said.

"Ten thousand dollars appeared in her bank account two days ago."

"Just to keep an eye on the apartment, I presume?"

"Yes."

"Did you find any connection between them?"

"In a chat room for single moms, I found a private message, saying that he can help her out. That he was a goodwill kind of guy, and he just wanted to keep an eye on the apartment. He paid her ten grand to watch Tabi's apartment for a week."

"And, of course, she said yes." He remembered the security system video of her scampering back across the hallway to her apartment. "So maybe it's not of any value to contact her."

"Chat line, bank deposit, all anonymous," she said. "No reporting required, so that was the end of the conversation."

"So another dead end."

"But it also shows how much care he's taking."

"Right. I thought about checking into the hotel staff, to see if we have any other turncoats here."

"Don't bother," she said. "Stone's been swearing at that database for hours. He just got in a little bit ago."

"Anything?"

"If there is, I'll let you know." And she hung up.

Just before the alarms went off at six, Eton and Cain were both up and came over just as the coffee rolled up outside the door. They moved the trolley into the room and came to sit beside Ryland. "Find out anything?"

"Stone hacked into the hotel database and couldn't find any connection to us here. It looks like we might be safe." He told them about the woman in the apartment across from Tabi's.

"So," Eton said, "a single mom just looking to make a little bit of money, probably scared, but, at the same time, hoping she has nothing more to do with them."

"Stone's still looking to see if they can find any other

connections, but, so far, it looks like a dead end," Cain added.

"I hope he doesn't clean up after himself on that one," Ryland said, not wanting the death of a single mom on his conscience.

"Let's make sure he doesn't," Cain added thoughtfully, "by taking him down later today."

They all sucked back their coffee, waiting for an alert from the rest of the team.

When it came in, Ryland looked at the message on his phone and read it aloud with satisfaction. *"Everything in place."* He reached down, pulled the sim card from his phone, and snapped it in half. The other two men did the same. Then with the disposable phones that they had brought, they quickly synched up each other's new numbers. He walked over and picked up Tabi's phone, pulled the sim card from it, and gave her a burner phone too. He didn't snap her sim; he just left it for her.

"You don't want to break it?" Eton said.

"Not if I don't have to," he replied.

Eton nodded in understanding.

"Good luck keeping her calm and quiet today," Cain added.

"Only until ten," Ryland said. "Then we'll see you at the museum."

"You decided to go yourself?" Eton asked.

"I might as well," Ryland said. "Who knows? We do these kind of security jobs all the time. Plus, I have a connection to Malcolm, who'll be running the private security for the tour. We already have an established relationship."

"Makes sense," Eton said, and, with that, Cain and Eton

quickly inhaled thick protein shakes, sucked back the last of the coffee, and said, "We're out."

Cain added before leaving, "Remember. We take them all alive."

Ryland watched them both go, and, as soon as the door closed, Tabi rose from the bed.

CHAPTER 14

TABI SAT UP slowly, looked at Ryland, and asked, "So, is it all set up?"

"It is," he said. "They'll do a run-through right now and check out the lay of the land. The rest of the team is in place."

"You're putting a lot on this, taking a chance that they'll come after me."

"No," he said. "But I'll sweeten the pot because I'm coming with you, as me."

She stared at him in understanding, and he appreciated it. Then her face pinched, and she whispered, "Of course you are."

"Remember? The bigger pot of gold we bring in, the more chance Green'll take the bait."

"And, of course, Green already knows the rest of your team is here."

"Yeah, they all used their real passports to land," he said cheerfully.

She groaned. "How much time do we have?"

"It's seven-thirty right now," he said. "We'll leave at nine-thirty."

"Good," she said, as she got up and went to the bathroom. By the time she came back out, he lifted the pot of coffee, only it was empty. She frowned and said, "Do we get more?"

"More and breakfast," he said.

"I love this hotel," she cried out joyfully. Sitting down, she looked outside and said, "It's raining out."

"It does rain here," he said mildly.

"True. Very true. Still, it just seems like a bad omen or something."

"It's better cover actually," he said. "For us and for them."

"I'm still not happy about it," she announced.

"Doesn't matter either way," he said. "It's the cards we have to deal with." When his phone buzzed, he said, "Breakfast is outside."

She sighed, hopped to her feet, and raced to the door, then hesitated.

He smiled and said, "I'm coming too." He got up, walked over, and opened the door. Once again, it was just the trolley.

"My nerves are so on edge," she murmured. "I half expected people to jump through the doors, guns blazing."

"You missed out on all that," he said, chuckling.

"I know, but somehow it all still has that edge to it."

By the time they ate, she was dressed and ready to go. She stopped at the doorway, looked at him, and said, "You'll look after yourself, right?"

"Of course," he said.

She frowned. "No unnecessary risks. And remember. You're already hurt."

He reached out, tapped her lips slightly, and said, "Remember? That's not part of this."

"It is part of this," she said. "I don't want you to get any more hurt than you already are."

He leaned over and kissed her gently and said, "Neither do I. Besides we have a sailboat to buy and a trip to take."

"Promise?"

"I promise," he said, as he slipped his arms around her and held her close for a long moment. Then he stepped back and said, "Come on. It's time to go."

IT WAS CALM and quiet as Ryland and Tabi walked casually down the street. When they arrived at the museum, they walked up the steps where Malcolm awaited Ryland. With a big smile the two men shook hands, and Ryland introduced Tabi. She smiled, tilted her head regally, and they walked inside.

Malcolm turned to Ryland, with a smile. "Man, you know how to bring trouble, don't you?"

"I know how to get into trouble too, apparently," he said.

Tabi chuckled and said, "You got that right."

Malcolm looked at her and said, "I heard something about you saving his life."

Such a note of admiration was in his tone that Ryland wanted to knock him back. "She did," he said, putting an arm possessively around her shoulders.

Tabi smiled at Malcolm. "I was just at the right place at the right time."

"Sometimes that's all it takes," he said with a serious tone.

As they walked into the museum, Ryland leaned ever-so-slightly forward and said to Tabi, "Remember. Stay alert. Also Malcolm will be out of here soon, and he'll be whisked back, so he's safe."

She shrugged. "There's enough people involved." He looked at her and frowned, then turned and left her standing in front of a particularly obscure piece of bronze. She walked around it, as if trying to figure out what it was. He had no idea himself. He would read the title later and hopefully an explanation would be found. Meanwhile he walked back to Malcolm. "Aren't you leaving?"

He shook his head. "I've been requested to stay."

Ryland frowned. "It could get very dangerous."

"So I've been told," he said, with a hard look. "Like I said, you know how to bring trouble."

"You got a place to hole up?"

"Got an office."

"I suggest you go find it for an hour."

Malcolm looked undecided, but Ryland said, "Look. We've got a lot of men here. We don't want a stray bullet to catch you."

"Okay," he said. "You got my number. Text me when I can come out."

"Will do," he said. He waited and watched as Malcolm turned and walked away. Then he walked back to Tabi. "Happy?"

She didn't look up from reading the sign on the base of the statute. "Much better," she said. "The fewer people who get hurt in this, the better."

"Says you," he said.

She looked at him. "I like him. He's nice."

He just rolled his eyes at her.

She chuckled and pointed at the plaque. "Do you ever wonder how stuff like this makes it in the art world?"

"What is it?"

"It's called, 'Eruptions of Thought,'" she said. "Looks

like a volcanic eruption gone wrong."

He chuckled at that too. "Come on," he said. "Let's stroll around slowly." They walked around, commenting on the various art pieces. He thoroughly enjoyed hearing her mind come up with some of the most bizarre suggestions for what stuff really was. "You're not really an art person, are you?"

"I know it's trite to say," she said. "However, I like what I like, but I don't really know why."

"I think even if you know that much, it helps," he said, as they walked through into a large selection of massive paintings.

She walked up to one that just had a single black dot. It was at the eleven o'clock mark if looking at the face of a clock. "I don't get it," she said.

"It's titled, 'With a Question Mark.' Does that help?"

At that, she burst out laughing. "Somebody probably made fifty grand for that." She cast a last look at it, then turned and walked toward some others.

He kept looking around, hearing everything. Finally a tap came on his intercom. *Alert.* He walked over and slipped his hand in hers, so he could grasp her fingers and said, "Company's coming."

She stiffened and then relaxed. "Good," she said. "That's what we wanted."

"It is, indeed," he murmured. They continued to walk, much more alert and aware, but she didn't appear to give any notice that anything was amiss. He really appreciated that about her. "You're really good under tough circumstances."

"I'm a surgical nurse," she said. "Tough circumstances? That's what we do. Quite often anyway."

He thought about that and realized how true it was. "Do

you lose many?"

"Not if I can help it," she said. "Sometimes the person is already all but gone before we even begin. Sometimes things happen during surgery, you know? Like, if their heart stops. Sometimes they can have a full-blown heart attack while they're in there. Sometimes it's something that we didn't even have any idea about, and, when we open them up to do one thing, we find they're completely riddled with something else. Again you just never know."

She pointed to a large wooden carving in the center. It was like a big circle with the top twisted up, almost in an inverted heart shape. "See? Now I like that one," she said.

"But what do you like about it?"

"I love the texture of the wood. I love the softness. I love the almost eroticism of it maybe," she said, standing here. "As if we're both independent but are coming together, by will."

He smiled and teased, "A romantic."

"We all are, actually," she said. "Just different variations of it. We all want a happily ever after. We all want to grow old and have that rocking chair on the porch. Still in good health and regaling our grandkids with tales of our glory days," she said with a laugh.

"I can't think of anything I'd like better," he said, as they kept walking, hand in hand.

A few minutes later she whispered, "Still nothing?"

"You won't know," he said. "If we're lucky, neither one of us will see him."

"That won't happen," she said, as they turned to look at a piece that seemed to change colors.

Then he got a quick code. *Move.* "Move into the next room," he told her, pushing her along quickly, then stationing her behind a big statue, as Ryland listened for further comm, while checking out the room.

Tabi had a few tense moments; then Ryland gave her the all clear.

"For the moment," she whispered.

A vent above them opened, and a gunman dropped down in front of them.

It was Green.

He carried a Glock in one hand and a semiautomatic in the other. He smiled and said, "There you are."

CHAPTER 15

T ABI STARED AT him in shock. "Where did you come from?" And damn it, her voice squeaked, like she was a petrified little girl. But, then again, she was feeling little, for this was one thing in theory and an entirely different thing in reality.

Green just smiled and said, "Innocent is what you were before you hooked up with this guy—but not now."

"So are you the asshole who blew up the plane and dropped us into the water?" Ryland asked.

"One of them," he said.

She felt Ryland stiffen at her side. "One of them?" he said, his voice harsh.

A second gunman appeared.

"Yep, we're a team," Green said, including his partner with a quick hand gesture. "We took out the three of you, right in the beginning, but unfortunately it looks like we only got one. I don't understand how you evaded that."

Then Green pointed the gun toward Tabi. "But they wouldn't have except for you. You saved them. I had an eye on them from a distance, a long way away," he said. "I knew where they were because we had a drone go over them. We were hoping they would just sink and drown. I was trying to get a boat, so I could finish the job. Then you arrived. Not only did you arrive but you brought the US Navy into it."

She stared at him in horror. "So, what? You would go drown them, even after you blew them out of the air?"

"Damn right I would," he said with disgust. "The job's not done, until it's done."

"And that means you've got somebody after Garret right now?"

"Or maybe multiple somebodies," he said, with a sly smile.

"Well, before we die, don't I have the right to know why?" Tabi asked.

"Well, you get to die because you hooked up with this guy. That's all it is—wrong place at the wrong time."

"And I don't get any time off for good behavior, huh?" At the corner of her eye, she caught a flash of black. She hoped that was Cain or Eton. And that's when it settled into her, deep inside, knowing that she and Ryland really weren't alone.

Green looked at her, startled, and said, "Good behavior? No, not when you're working for the wrong team."

"I didn't realize there *was* a team," she said sadly. "Whatever happened to live and let live?"

"I intend to do just that," he said. "But not right now. Not until we're done with this bullshit."

"You still haven't explained *why*. What is this even about?"

"You know something? That's enough talking. You're stalling, and I don't have time for that shit." He lifted his gun and pointed it a little bit higher, toward her. She cried out and ducked to the side. He laughed and aimed again and got tackled from the back by Cain, just as Ryland slammed into Green from the front, while Eton took on Green's partner in a highly coordinated attack.

Green's gun went off harmlessly into the floor, as she dashed around that big wooden carving. She grabbed a hold of it, wishing it were wider, so she could hide behind it. It was open in the center, and, just when she thought this fight was about to be done, two quick gunshots went off, and she watched Ryland jolt with the blows.

She cried out and raced forward, even as Green dropped to the floor with a bloody wound to show for it. And another gun fired again, this time at her. She dove to the ground, snagging the handgun the first guy, Green, had dropped, and she rolled, pointed the Glock at the second shooter, and fired. He went down, and she immediately turned the gun on a third shooter. *Where the hell did he come from?* Then froze, when the gunman pointed a semiautomatic at her. She had a handgun pointed at him, and both Ryland and Cain were on the ground. Only Ryland appeared to be bleeding. Then she thought she caught a glimpse of Eton, but too far away …

The third gunman whispered, "Let it go. You'll never shoot me, not in time."

"No, maybe not," she said, with a brave smile. "But, if I shoot you, even if you do shoot me," she said, "you won't get to kill these good men." And she smiled at him as she talked, knowing that he would watch her gun hand and would moderate any changes in her voice, so she kept it steady and low.

"Besides, isn't it time for this to be over?" She lowered the gun, as if giving up, then fired from the hip. He took the blow in his gut, even as Ryland kicked away the semiautomatic, but it fired at the same time the gunman went down, even as she got to her feet. Cain was up now, holding a handgun on Green and the third gunman, both on the floor, both slowly bleeding out.

She walked over slowly to Green, down, bleeding, still alive, and asked him, "Why?"

"Why?" He tried to speak, his voice gasping, as blood and air bubbled up freely from his gaping chest wound.

She looked at him dispassionately. The nurse in her said to help him.

But the victim in her, who had already been shot at, who had watched him blow a plane out of the air, trying to kill defenseless men, and knowing he'd sat and watched Ryland and Garret struggle to live, just waiting for them to slip into the water and die, was quite prepared to let him choke out.

Just then she heard a heavy guttural groan beside her, and she turned to see Ryland on his knees, a hand against his shoulder.

She raced to his side, pulled his hand back. "Lay down flat now," she barked.

He looked at her in surprise, but, instead of lying down, he slowly keeled over.

Cain called out, "How bad?"

"Shot in the lung," she snapped. "We need a medic, right now."

The next ten minutes were organized chaos, as she ripped open Ryland's jacket to find a bulletproof vest, which she then had to find a way under and around, to get to the chest wound that was sucking air out, even as she worked. "Damn. Armor-piercing bullets," she said to anyone close enough to hear. She slapped her palm over the hole and said, "I need a piece of plastic."

Cain looked at her in surprise.

"I don't care where you get it from," she said. "I need a sheet of flexible plastic now."

Cain nodded to Eton, his target already dead. When Eton returned a moment later, she recognized it as a piece of plastic packing material that had probably once wrapped a big art piece.

She nodded and slapped it against the open wound on Ryland's chest. Immediately it sucked in, sealing off the lung. "Did you call it in?"

"Ambulance is on the way," Eton said, as he knelt beside Ryland and said, "That's two gunshot wounds for him."

"He's out of action now for sure," she said. "I don't know what else you've got going on after this, but Ryland needs time to heal."

"I know," Cain said, as he looked at her. "Listen," he said. "We can't be here."

She looked up at him, nodding, instinctively understanding what he was saying.

"The second gunman is dead. Nice shooting, by the way. I'll check the third one and see if we need anything from him," Cain said. "I've already stripped Green and the second one clean."

"Will you take them away?" she asked.

"No," he said, "but I'll call in people to make sure this is cleaned up."

She gave him a weak smile. "Says you."

"I promise."

She looked up at him, seeing the sincerity in his voice. "Is the third gunman dead?"

He walked over and said, "Not yet. But a stomach wound is a painful way to die."

"Well, I'm working on the one I plan to save," she said. "Green and his remaining buddy can die, for all I care."

The victim in front of Cain tried to speak, and she

watched as Cain knelt down in front of the guy, the weapons cleared away from him. The man reached out, grabbed his vest, and, even from where she sat, she heard it, as he whispered to Cain, "You're next."

Cain immediately straightened as the man gave a large gasping rattle and died. He walked back to her and said, "No, he's not alive."

She nodded and said, "Don't think I didn't hear that."

"I know," he said. "You'll tell Ryland, as soon as he's awake. But, in the meantime, I'm taking the team, and I'm leaving."

She looked up at him. "Do you think there're any other bad guys?"

"They got one at the hospital, trying for Garret. He was intercepted in the underground parking area. No one else here. My men have checked."

Her eyebrows raised. "Good, you'll need guards for both of them now. You know that, right?"

"How long will Ryland be down?"

"With that lung, hard to say. A month anyway? It'll heal, but he won't have his capacity or strength for quite a while. Like I said, he's out. He's also been hit in the shoulder. He can't carry a weapon for a long time."

"What are your plans?"

"Get him to the hospital, get him fixed up, and go get a sailboat," she said. "Hopefully all within a few weeks."

He smiled. "You'll stay in touch? You know that the minute he's conscious, he'll want to start running command central," he said. "That much he can do. But—keep in touch and let us know how he is."

She nodded, Cain full well knowing she would take off and nurse Ryland back to health, no matter how long it took.

With that, he checked on Green on his way out. "Green's dead."

"Good," she said, as Cain started to walk away. "Cain?"

He turned to give her a look. "Look after yourself," she said, with one eyebrow raised. Then added with a smile, "Ryland will heal much faster if he knows that the rest of you are okay."

"I thought so," he said, with a bark of laughter. "Will do." And, with that, he disappeared.

She heard the sirens coming up from the back alley. She pulled out Ryland's phone, found Malcolm's number, and called him. When he answered, she said, "Get up here. Ryland's been shot twice. We've got three dead bodies, and the ambulance is coming." Then she dropped the phone, as she worked to staunch the bleeding from Ryland's shoulder wound. By the time Malcolm raced to her side, she said, "Good timing. Now you've got to come up with a cover story for yourself."

He looked at her, looked at the dead gunmen, and swore.

"I know, but Ryland needs emergency medical help. And, if Ryland's team had taken the bodies, there would still be pools of blood, and then what would we do? Cain did say he was calling in people to clean up."

"This will just be what, a random attack?"

"We'll say they were after the museum. The IT is being upgraded, and they used this opportunity to get in and check out what was worth taking. They were scoping it out and, when we came in for our private showing, we surprised them, and they attacked us."

He looked at her in admiration. "You know what? That

just might work," he said.

"By the time I phone the governor on Ryland's behalf," she said, "it will work."

The paramedics came, beating on the doors, as Malcolm opened them up and led them right to her. Three of them split off to look at the dead men and then came back to her.

She already had Ryland up and loaded on a gurney. "Let's go. Let's go. Let's go," she said.

She raced out to the ambulance, giving Malcolm a hard look as they left. The cops were already here, and she knew that somebody up high enough would be briefed on the scenario. Hopefully she had just made Malcolm's life a little easier, rather than having it appear that he hadn't been there, doing his job. She didn't want that to happen.

Thinking about that, she grabbed Ryland's phone again, realizing it was the burner with not much on it, and hoping like hell he'd put the governor's number in it. She didn't know who the hell he'd called, but he had several missed calls. Ice was in there and several others. Finally she saw George and hit the button. She recognized the governor's voice immediately. "This is Tabi, with an update on Ryland."

"What happened?"

"Chaos," she said. "The good guys won, but we need your help." She quickly gave him an outline on what was going on.

"I heard from Cain," he said. "He's coming in on my other line."

"Good," she said. "I'm on the way to the hospital right now with Ryland."

"Will he make it?"

"If I have any say in the matter, he will, yes," she said

and hung up.

RYLAND WOKE TO the sounds of machinery and a weird smell and something stuffed up his nostrils and definitely silence, outside of this weird humming machine. He stared at the ceiling and then at the machine. "So it's a hospital," he murmured to himself.

"Yes," Tabi said. "My hospital."

He smiled, as he slowly rotated his head to the other side. And there she was, tired and exhausted, yet valiant. The fact that he was awake and talking had put a smile on her face at least. She stood, leaned over, and kissed him gently on the cheek. "Well, the good guys won," she said. "And you're the only casualty on our team."

"That's good. Is Malcolm okay?"

"Malcolm's just fine," she said. "Cain's fine too, and so is the rest of the team. They took out one of the bad guys in the hospital's underground parking lot, trying to get to Garret, and the three inside the museum."

"Yes, I remember that part. And, lady, you are a fine shot. Where did you learn to do that?"

"I didn't do anything but point and shoot," she said. "I'll take it as a miracle that I actually hit them."

"You did just fine," he murmured. "How badly am I hurt?"

"Lung," she said. "Which I managed to get sealed up pretty quickly. You're through the surgery already, and you have a pretty bad bullet wound in the shoulder too, so you'll be out for weeks."

"And you made sure of that, didn't you?" he said with a smile in his voice.

"Well, I did agree that you could run control after this."

His eyes flew open, and he looked at her with interest.

"But you can't go running around all across the world until your body heals. All those fractures are still not setting properly because you won't give your body a chance to heal right."

"I can run command central?" he asked, looking on the import of this. "It'll take me a bit to update it with all the rest of the information."

"You can do that tomorrow," she said. "Right now, you're getting more medication, more painkillers, and you'll go back to sleep again."

Even as he protested, he felt the words turning into a yawn, and he rolled over and quickly fell asleep again.

The next time he woke up, she was there again. "Did you sleep?"

"As much as anybody can in a chair," she said.

He looked at her and said, "News?"

"All kinds of it. I've been running your phone and making phone calls myself. I think that you missed the last part after I shot the third gunman," she said. "He said that Cain's next."

At that, Ryland's face sharpened. "Is he okay?"

"I haven't heard from him," she admitted. "But he took off out of there with the rest of the team."

"I know how to contact them," he said. "I'm feeling great, so can I have my laptop?"

She looked at him, sighed, and said, "No point in saying no because I know you'll just worry and fret about your friends."

"*Fret*, really?" he said in disgust. "That sounds like a little old lady."

"And that's the role you're locked into, right now," she warned. "At least until we get you all healed up and strong again."

"I can't run the electronics I need to from here," he said.

She sat at the edge of the bed and asked, "Where do you need to go to do that?"

He looked at her, smiled, and said, "I've got an idea."

"I don't think I like the look on your face," she said.

"But you'll love this," he said. "Can you take more time off?"

"The hospital has already okayed it," she said, "because no way I would let you go back out there again. Somebody had to make sure you stayed alive and well."

"How long do we have?"

"Two weeks at the moment," she said, with a shrug.

He picked up his phone and asked, "How bad is my lung?"

"You're not doing bad," she said. "As long as all we'll do is laze around."

"How about float around?"

She stared at him in surprise and then said, "What do you have in mind?"

CHAPTER 16

W HAT RYLAND HAD in mind was a sailboat off the coast. And Tabi still didn't understand how quickly they'd gotten here. He'd had himself medevacked out to a coastal town, with her at his side. She had all the medicines they needed in a bag, and he had been transported in a wheelchair and led her toward a large sailboat.

Now safely aboard, she walked around the deck and smiled. He sat in a lawn chair with a laptop and satellite hookups, electronic equipment all around him. "How did you make all this happen in five hours?" she asked.

"It's my world," he said. "I make things happen. That's what I do."

She shook her head. "Freaking amazing." She walked to the mast and leaned against it, staring at the blue waters all around.

"Will this do?"

"It will for a little bit," she said, laughing. "As long as nobody knows where we are, and we won't get attacked from the sky."

"We shouldn't. Ice has Stone running proxies right now."

"Whatever that means," she said. "Did you find Cain?"

He looked up and flashed her a bright smile. "Yes, he's gone underground to regroup."

"Perfect, and Garret's still in the hospital," she said. "I just heard from the surgeon. Apparently he's showing signs that he's starting to stir a little bit."

"Now that is perfect," he said.

She smiled, knowing how hard and fast the road had been to get them to where they were. Then she noticed the white pinched look around his mouth. "Time to put it away and go lie down for a bit," she said.

His lips tightened, as if he would protest; then he relaxed and nodded. "You're right. Can you help me move this stuff to one side?" Soon they had everything secured and in the locked waterproof boxes that were set up all around. With that done, he slowly got up, and, with her help, they managed to get him below to the bed.

As he laid down, he said, "You could join me."

"I could," she said, with a smile. "As long as there's no hanky-panky because I can't risk having you hurt."

"You're such a pain," he murmured.

"I am," she said, laughing, as she leaned over and kissed him. But, when she went to pull away, he grabbed her head, then pulled her down and kissed her hard. She shook her head. "You're too injured for this."

"Maybe," he murmured. "But not if I don't have to do any of the work."

She stared at him in surprise and delight. "Oh, don't tell me that you'll just lie there and let me do my worst?"

"I would love nothing more," he said. Since he already wore swim shorts, and she was in a bikini top and bottoms, it was much easier to strip down. He had his shorts off in seconds, lying here, completely bare and waiting for anything she wanted to do.

As she sat down, her bikini long gone, she said, "You

know something? I don't think I've ever had this opportunity before."

He looked at her curiously. "What do you mean?"

"Not too many men are just happy to lie there and do nothing."

"Well, I can't promise to continue doing nothing," he said, "but you've definitely got a chance to get started." And with a suggestive wink, he said, "Do your worst."

She shook her head. "No, I'll take it easy on you," she said. "After all, you're injured."

"I'm not *that* injured," he protested.

She leaned over and kissed him again. When he went to grab her head, she shook her head and placed his hands down beside him and said, "Don't move." Delight lit the dark depths of his gaze as she ran her fingers across his features, dropping kisses on his brows and his nose, stroking her fingers through his hair. "I almost lost you," she murmured and dropped her cheek against his for a long moment. Then she kissed him again and again. She climbed up, so she straddled his body, her hands gently stroking across his heavily muscular chest and shoulders.

With misgivings, she stared at the bandages on his shoulder from one of the latest bullet wounds, until he reached up and said, "Don't stop. I'm fine."

"Fine you are not," she said, "but I'll go easy."

She gently whispered her fingers across his skin, exploring and finding out who he was on the outside, since she already knew exactly who he was on the inside. He was honorable, loyal, caring, and dedicated; he was all of that and more. And, on the outside, he was such a warrior. She flicked his nipples with her nails and ran her fingers in a circle around and across his chest, seeing the other bullet wound there. She swallowed back her tears, then she rubbed upward, massaging his muscles as she moved up and down his chest and belly. She scampered a little lower, so she could explore where his ribs rose. His belly dropped immediately at her light touch; his six-pack rose at her tickling.

He gasped and said, "Well, that won't go down well."

She leaned over and kissed his belly button. "How about that though?" she murmured.

He groaned and said, "Okay, okay, I'll take some of that."

She let her hair, now free and long, drift across his erection, just a whisper of touch. He moaned, his hands still at his side, his hips twisting beneath her. She ran long smooth fingers down over his hip bones, to slide into the curls at the base of his growing erection, where she teased, tormented, and generally avoided the one area she knew he desperately wanted her to touch.

But she wasn't ready to give this up, and she knew that, when she did, it would be over, really fast. She stroked his thighs, the inside of which were supersoft, the hard quads, bigger and stronger than she could have imagined. But the calves on the man, she just shook her head when she came to his heavy foot. It was just unbelievable to see how much bigger and stronger than her that he was.

Slowly she made her way back up again, leaving a trail of kisses up and down his thighs. When she got to his hip, she moved to the inside of his hip bone, letting her hair once again drift and wrap around his proud member, as it stood higher. Then she grasped it gently with one hand and slowly stroked up and then down, exploring the firm ridge, the shape, and the texture. When she leaned over and kissed him on the tip, he roared, his hips coming up in a flash.

She smiled and let his penis drift between her breasts,

then momentarily hugged it with them, as she plumped her breasts around it, letting it slide lower and lower and lower, as she climbed up, until she slowly placed it at the heart of her and sank down. Immediately he thrust his hips up, groaning wildly. She smiled and shifted ever-so-slightly, leaning over so her hands were on the bed beside him.

"You know another activity I like to do?" she teased.

"This," he said desperately, his hips trying to plumb up and down inside her, but she wouldn't give him any space to do it.

"No," she said. "I like to ride." As she slowly lowered and raised herself, again and again, he grabbed her hips and held her as he lifted, finding the same rhythm, as she rode them right to the edge and hung there for a long moment.

When he grabbed her and pulled her down, plunging deeper and deeper and deeper, she cried out, as her world came crashing apart. He groaned beneath her and she sat still, on top of him, her head thrown back, as her arms collapsed against her thighs as she waited for all the trickles and rumbles of energy sliding up and down her body. Her nerve endings alive, awake, and screaming out in joy.

He reached up, slid his hands up her thighs, across her belly, up to cup her breasts, and he whispered, "God, woman, if you keep that up, you'll kill me yourself."

She smiled, looked at him, and said, "Yeah, but what a way to go."

He burst out laughing as she slowly lowered herself so that she was beside him.

"Now sleep," she whispered. "You really need it."

"Only if you sleep with me," he said. "It's been a pretty rough week for you too."

She kissed him gently on the cheek and said, "Yes, but it's over now. Now we have the rest of our lives."

EPILOGUE

CAIN BESTROW GRABBED his phone, saw the message from Ryland, and gave a small crow. "Apparently Garret's waking up," he said.

Eton was at his side and said, "Seriously?"

"He's not conscious yet, but they think he's coming out of it."

"That's huge," Eton said, as the two men high-fived each other. "Now the question is," Eton said, "what will we do about you?"

"We don't know jack shit yet," Cain said. "We've ID the three dead guys with Green—the two at the museum with him and the one at the hospital, heading for Garret. The guy at the hospital was a local, a gun for hire, we assume. But we've tracked the other two of Green's men back to Africa, but they were originally from Sicily."

"Sicily? Interesting," Eton said. "Have we had any cases there?"

"No, but that doesn't mean that somebody didn't hire the labor from over there."

"I know," Eton said. "I'm just trying to figure out what the connection is."

"Well," Cain said, "they're after all of us because Green's goon was very clear that I'm next."

"You think whoever's behind all this is intentionally

picking us off, one by one?" Eton asked.

"I think they're trying to," Cain said. "They were happy to take out three of us at the beginning—or maybe kill off the boss and whoever he's with—then go pick off the soldiers, one by one."

"That also implies that whoever is after us, is after all of us, and it's not just revenge against Bullard and his nameless team. This is more personal," Eton stated.

"Very," Cain said, just as another text came in. He read it, smiled, and said, "Ryland's doing better. He and Tabi are out on the sailboat right now, and he's running communications with Ice and Levi."

"Good," Eton said. "If anybody can keep track of us, it'll be Ryland. How bad are his injuries?"

"Doesn't matter," Cain said, "because you can count on the fact that Tabi won't let him die."

"Damn it. He sure lucked out, didn't he?" Eton said, a note of envy in his voice.

"He absolutely did," Cain said. "And she's got some spirit in her too. It's too bad she was already hooked on Ryland, or I might have made a move for her myself."

Eton chuckled. "No, I don't think there was any chance of that happening."

"So, since this asshole is after me next, it's up to me to figure out the next step."

"No," Eton said. "It's not. It's up to all of us. This isn't just about you. This is about the whole team. And we can't forget the fact that they might still decide to circle back around and take out Garret and Ryland."

"And maybe they will. We've still got security on Garret, and Tabi is no slouch, by any means. I still can't believe she killed that one gunman instantly with one shot."

"Beginner's luck? You know what they say about a lot of

women. It's instinctive for them to just point their finger, as they would at a naughty child. All they have to add is pulling the trigger to fire. Boom. There it is. It's a hell of a deal."

"Remember though, she killed another gunman with one shot too, just took longer for him to die."

"Amazing," Eton said.

"Well, I'm sure glad she was there," Cain said. "She also saved Ryland with her emergency nursing skills right in the first few minutes. If she hadn't sealed up that lung and controlled the bleeding, he never would have made it. She's the kind of person you need when it counts."

"Well, good for both of them," Eton said. "Now, what's next?"

Cain gave him a hard glance. "I guess I'll head for Sicily."

"Just because they were from there, doesn't mean that's where the trouble is."

"No, but that's where their connections will be. Somebody in Sicily will know who and where. So that's where I'm going."

"Okay then," Eton replied.

Cain looked at him. "You coming?"

"Hell yeah," Eton said. "You're not going there by yourself. That's for sure."

"Just the two of us though," Cain said. "Any more than that and we will attract more attention than we need. We made too much of a statement at the museum."

"Good," Eton said. "The statement the bad guys all need to know is that we've got their number and that we're coming for them, one by one."

This concludes Book 1 of Bullard's Battle: Ryland's Reach.

Read about Cain's Cross: Bullard's Battle, Book 2

Cain's Cross: Bullard's Battle (Book #2)

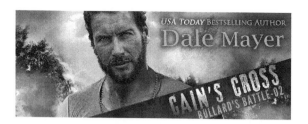

Welcome to a new stand-alone but interconnected series from Dale Mayer. This is Bullard's story—and that of his team's. All raw, rough, incredibly capable men who have one goal: to find out who was behind the attack on their leader, before the attacker, or attackers, return to finish the job.

Stay tuned for more nonstop action as the men narrow down their suspects ... and find a way to let love back into their own empty lives.

Cain—hearing a killer's last words, "You're next,"—knows his time is running out, not only for him but for his entire team. As members of his team search for the still missing Bullard in the ocean, Cain has focused on tracking the killer's history, hopefully to lead to the madman after them all. A trip to Sicily brings more information to light but also more puzzles to sort out. And an unexpected light in Cain's life.

When Petra picks up the two men at the airport, she has no idea how fast her personal life is about to unravel. Not only do these men bring up old terrible memories but they also shine a light on an ugly corner of town. People she avoids at all costs.

Still she can't afford to dwell on the past, as her present blows up. With Cain and Eton at her side, they're all trying to stay alive, as the bodies drop around them.

Find Book 2 here!
To find out more visit Dale Mayer's website.
smarturl.it/DMSCain

Damon's Deal: Terkel's Team (Book #1)

Welcome to a brand-new series from *USA Today* best-selling author Dale Mayer, where dark-ops SEALs have special senses and skills, needed to solve intrigue, betrayal, and … murder. A series with all the elements you've come to love, plus so much more, … including psychics!

ICE POURED HERSELF a coffee and sat down at the compound's massive dining room table with the others. When her phone rang, she smiled at the number displayed. "Hey, Terk. How're you doing?" She put the call on Speakerphone.

"I'm okay," Terkel said, his voice distracted and tight.

"Terk?" Merk called from across the table. He got up and walked closer and sat across from Levi. "You don't sound too good, brother. What's up?"

"I'm fine," Terk said. "Or I will be. Right now, things are blown to shit."

"As in literally?" Merk asked.

"The entire group," Terk said, "they're all gone. I had a solid team of eight, and they're all gone."

"Dead?"

Several others stood to join them, gathered around Ice's phone. Levi stepped forward, his hand on Ice's shoulder. "Terk? Are they all dead?"

"No." Terk took a deep breath. "I'm not making sense. I'm sorry."

"Take it easy," Ice said, her voice calm and reassuring. "What do you mean, *they're all gone?*"

"All their abilities are gone," he said. "Something's happened to them. Somebody has deliberately removed whatever super senses they could utilize—or what we have been utilizing for the last ten years for the government." His tone was bitter. "When the US gov recently closed us down, they promised that our black ops department would never rise again, but I didn't expect them to attack us personally."

"What are you talking about?" Merk said in alarm, standing up now to stare at Ice's phone. "Are you in danger?"

"Maybe? I don't know," Terk said. "I need to find out exactly what the hell's going on."

"What can we do to help?" Ice asked.

Terk gave a broken laugh. "That's not why I'm calling. Well, it is, but it isn't."

Ice looked at Merk, who frowned, as he shook his head. Ice knew he and the others had heard Terk's stressed out tone and the completely confusing bits and pieces coming from his mouth. Ice said, "Terk, you're not making sense again. Take a breath and explain. Please. You're scaring me."

Terk took a long slow deep breath. "Tell Stone to open the gate," he said. "She's out there."

"Who's out there?" Levi asked, hopped up, looked outside, and shrugged.

"She's coming up the road now. You have to let her in."

"Who? Why?"

"*Because*," he said, "she's also harnessed with C-4."

"Jesus," Levi said, bolting to display the camera feeds to the big screen in the room. "Is it live?"

"It is, and she's been sent to you."

"Well, that's an interesting move," Ice said, her voice sharp, activating her comm to connect to Stone in the control room. "Who's after us?"

"I think it's rebels within the Iranian government. But it could be our own government. I don't know anymore," Terk snapped. "I also don't know how they got her so close to you. Or how they pinned your connection to me," he said. "I've been very careful."

"We can look after ourselves," Ice said immediately. "But who is this woman to you?"

"She's pregnant," he said, "so that adds to the intensity here."

"Understood. So who is the father? Is he connected somehow?"

There was silence on the other end.

Merk said, "Terk, talk to us."

"She's carrying my baby," Terk replied, his voice heavy.

Merk, his expression grim, looked at Ice, her face mirroring his shock. He asked, "How do you know her, Terk?"

"Brother, you don't understand," Terk said. "I've never met this woman before in my life." And, with that, the phone went dead.

Find Book 1 here!

To find out more visit Dale Mayer's website.

smarturl.it/DMSTTDamon

Author's Note

Thank you for reading Ryland's Reach: Bullard's Battle, Book 1! If you enjoyed the book, please take a moment and leave a short review.

Dear reader,

I love to hear from readers, and you can contact me at my website: www.dalemayer.com or at my Facebook author page. To be informed of new releases and special offers, sign up for my newsletter or follow me on BookBub. And if you are interested in joining Dale Mayer's Reader Group, here is the Facebook sign up page.
https://smarturl.it/DaleMayerFBGroup

Cheers,
Dale Mayer

Get THREE Free Books Now!

Have you met the SEALS of Honor?

SEALs of Honor Books 1, 2, and 3. Follow the stories of brave, badass warriors who serve their country with honor and love their women to the limits of life and death.

Read Mason, Hawk, and Dane right now for FREE.

Go here and tell me where to send them!
http://smarturl.it/EthanBofB

About the Author

Dale Mayer is a *USA Today* best-selling author, best known for her SEALs military romances, her Psychic Visions series, and her Lovely Lethal Garden cozy series. Her contemporary romances are raw and full of passion and emotion (Broken But … Mending series). Her thrillers will keep you guessing (By Death series), and her romantic comedies will keep you giggling (*It's a Dog's Life*, a stand-alone novella; and the Broken Protocols series, starring Charming Marvin, the cat).

Dale honors the stories that come to her—and some of them are crazy and break all the rules and cross multiple genres!

To go with her fiction, she also writes nonfiction in many different fields, with books available on résumé writing, companion gardening, and the US mortgage system. She has recently published her Career Essentials series. All her books are available in print and ebook format.

Connect with Dale Mayer Online

Dale's Website – www.dalemayer.com
Twitter – @DaleMayer
Facebook – facebook.com/DaleMayer.author
BookBub – bookbub.com/authors/dale-mayer

Also by Dale Mayer

Published Adult Books:

Bullard's Battle

Ryland's Reach, Book 1

Cain's Cross, Book 2

Eton's Escape, Book 3

Garret's Gambit, Book 4

Kano's Keep, Book 5

Fallon's Flaw, Book 6

Quinn's Quest, Book 7

Bullard's Beauty, Book 8

Bullard's Best, Book 9

Terkel's Team

Damon's Deal, Book 1

Kate Morgan

Simon Says... Hide, Book 1

Hathaway House

Aaron, Book 1

Brock, Book 2

Cole, Book 3

Denton, Book 4

Elliot, Book 5

Finn, Book 6

Gregory, Book 7

Heath, Book 8

Iain, Book 9

Jaden, Book 10

Keith, Book 11

Lance, Book 12

Melissa, Book 13

Nash, Book 14

Owen, Book 15

Hathaway House, Books 1–3

Hathaway House, Books 4–6

Hathaway House, Books 7–9

The K9 Files

Ethan, Book 1

Pierce, Book 2

Zane, Book 3

Blaze, Book 4

Lucas, Book 5

Parker, Book 6

Carter, Book 7

Weston, Book 8

Greyson, Book 9

Rowan, Book 10

Caleb, Book 11

Kurt, Book 12

Tucker, Book 13

Harley, Book 14

The K9 Files, Books 1–2

The K9 Files, Books 3–4

The K9 Files, Books 5–6

The K9 Files, Books 7–8

The K9 Files, Books 9–10

The K9 Files, Books 11–12

Lovely Lethal Gardens

Arsenic in the Azaleas, Book 1

Bones in the Begonias, Book 2

Corpse in the Carnations, Book 3

Daggers in the Dahlias, Book 4

Evidence in the Echinacea, Book 5

Footprints in the Ferns, Book 6

Gun in the Gardenias, Book 7

Handcuffs in the Heather, Book 8

Ice Pick in the Ivy, Book 9

Jewels in the Juniper, Book 10

Killer in the Kiwis, Book 11

Lifeless in the Lilies, Book 12

Murder in the Marigolds, Book 13

Lovely Lethal Gardens, Books 1–2

Lovely Lethal Gardens, Books 3–4

Lovely Lethal Gardens, Books 5–6

Lovely Lethal Gardens, Books 7–8

Lovely Lethal Gardens, Books 9–10

Psychic Vision Series

Tuesday's Child

Hide 'n Go Seek

Maddy's Floor

Garden of Sorrow

Knock Knock…

Rare Find

Eyes to the Soul

Now You See Her

Shattered

Into the Abyss

Seeds of Malice

Eye of the Falcon

Itsy-Bitsy Spider

Unmasked

Deep Beneath

From the Ashes

Stroke of Death

Ice Maiden

Snap, Crackle…

Psychic Visions Books 1–3

Psychic Visions Books 4–6

Psychic Visions Books 7–9

By Death Series

Touched by Death

Haunted by Death

Chilled by Death

By Death Books 1–3

Broken Protocols – Romantic Comedy Series

Cat's Meow

Cat's Pajamas

Cat's Cradle

Cat's Claus

Broken Protocols 1-4

Broken and... Mending

Skin

Scars

Scales (of Justice)

Broken but... Mending 1-3

Glory

Genesis

Tori

Celeste

Glory Trilogy

Biker Blues

Morgan: Biker Blues, Volume 1

Cash: Biker Blues, Volume 2

SEALs of Honor

Mason: SEALs of Honor, Book 1

Hawk: SEALs of Honor, Book 2

Dane: SEALs of Honor, Book 3

Swede: SEALs of Honor, Book 4

Shadow: SEALs of Honor, Book 5

Cooper: SEALs of Honor, Book 6

Markus: SEALs of Honor, Book 7

Evan: SEALs of Honor, Book 8

Mason's Wish: SEALs of Honor, Book 9

Chase: SEALs of Honor, Book 10

Brett: SEALs of Honor, Book 11

Devlin: SEALs of Honor, Book 12

Easton: SEALs of Honor, Book 13

Ryder: SEALs of Honor, Book 14

Macklin: SEALs of Honor, Book 15

Corey: SEALs of Honor, Book 16

Warrick: SEALs of Honor, Book 17

Tanner: SEALs of Honor, Book 18

Jackson: SEALs of Honor, Book 19

Kanen: SEALs of Honor, Book 20

Nelson: SEALs of Honor, Book 21

Taylor: SEALs of Honor, Book 22

Colton: SEALs of Honor, Book 23

Troy: SEALs of Honor, Book 24

Axel: SEALs of Honor, Book 25

Baylor: SEALs of Honor, Book 26

SEALs of Honor, Books 1–3

SEALs of Honor, Books 4–6

SEALs of Honor, Books 7–10

SEALs of Honor, Books 11–13

SEALs of Honor, Books 14–16

SEALs of Honor, Books 17–19

SEALs of Honor, Books 20–22

SEALs of Honor, Books 23–25

Heroes for Hire

Shane, Book 12

Diesel, Book 13

Jerricho, Book 14

The Mavericks, Books 1–2

The Mavericks, Books 3–4

The Mavericks, Books 5–6

The Mavericks, Books 7–8

The Mavericks, Books 9–10

The Mavericks, Books 11–12

Collections

Dare to Be You...

Dare to Love...

Dare to be Strong...

RomanceX3

Standalone Novellas

It's a Dog's Life

Riana's Revenge

Second Chances

Published Young Adult Books:

Family Blood Ties Series

Vampire in Denial

Vampire in Distress

Vampire in Design

Vampire in Deceit

Vampire in Defiance

Vampire in Conflict

Vampire in Chaos

Vampire in Crisis

Vampire in Control

Vampire in Charge

Family Blood Ties Set 1–3

Family Blood Ties Set 1–5

Family Blood Ties Set 4–6

Family Blood Ties Set 7–9

Sian's Solution, A Family Blood Ties Series Prequel
   Novelette

Design series

Dangerous Designs

Deadly Designs

Darkest Designs

Design Series Trilogy

Standalone

In Cassie's Corner

Gem Stone (a Gemma Stone Mystery)

Time Thieves

Published Non-Fiction Books:

Career Essentials

Career Essentials: The Résumé

Career Essentials: The Cover Letter

Career Essentials: The Interview

Career Essentials: 3 in 1

Made in the USA
Columbia, SC
21 May 2022